About the Author

The author was born in a coastal town in Albania, where he attended hotel school. His passion for books and reading led him to write his first book when he was only twenty years old. Now, he lives in Europe with his family, following his passion for writing.

In the Name of Imagination

V. M. Dada

In the Name of Imagination

Olympia Publishers
London

www.olympiapublishers.com
OLYMPIA PAPERBACK EDITION

Copyright © **V. M. Dada 2024**

The right of V. M. Dada to be identified as author of
this work has been asserted in accordance with sections 77 and 78 of
the Copyright, Designs and Patents Act 1988.

All Rights Reserved

No reproduction, copy or transmission of this publication
may be made without written permission.
No paragraph of this publication may be reproduced,
copied or transmitted save with the written permission of the publisher,
or in accordance with the provisions
of the Copyright Act 1956 (as amended).

Any person who commits any unauthorised act in relation to
this publication may be liable to criminal
prosecution and civil claims for damage.

A CIP catalogue record for this title is
available from the British Library.

ISBN: 978-1-80439-674-2

This is a work of fiction.
Names, characters, places and incidents originate from the writer's
imagination. Any resemblance to actual persons, living or dead, is
purely coincidental.

First Published in 2024

Olympia Publishers
Tallis House
2 Tallis Street
London
EC4Y 0AB

Printed in Great Britain

Dedication

For Amelia.

Acknowledgements

I thank my family for the support to continue this difficult path, as well as the person of life for the suggestions and help given in her opinions to clothe a book in the most adequate form.

Illusion

My eyes were closed because I wanted to enter the tranquility of sleep, but I was consumed in the clutches of imagination. What came to my mind in an imagination where the main condition was clean images that make me smile and feel good. Everything seemed to me like a reality in two parallelisms, where one called me to open my eyes, the other to close them. The confusion was colossal when it came to spontaneous thoughts of the brain that I did not know what to call, so, with the greatest fear and the least prejudice, I decided to enter the reality of open eyes.

I opened my eyes and was directly faced with a strong, blinding light. I was sitting on a beautiful couch that filled a special corner that I had bought just a few days before, but not above the couch, below it. In the world I imagined, existence was omnipresent, wearing a gray cloak that imposed deception and anything could happen, but it couldn't be as it seemed, at least not like me and her lying on the floor, in its coldness, and with the blazing fire in front of it that warmed the room and our hearts, and with the feeble rays of light that entered the room all lazily as if someone were forcing it to do its duty.

That weak and strained ray of light came through our slightly open windows, where the curtains flapped, making them look like an imaginary wave of the sea. I sat, lost, and thought about the way that light has traveled here on her face, in our bodies, the clock that marked 14:23 minutes, in this room where there is a need for the lights more than ever, even though the natural lighting was present everywhere, but we wanted more, we wanted everything more, we also wanted love in high doses, when in reality we only took as much as our body allowed us, best coping with the demonstrative control of metabolism.

I opened my eyes and got out of the hypnotic sleep that had captured me, or rather I tried to get out... I got out. With my eyes, I saw that she was there, looking at me strangely without speaking, seeing the sweat flowing from my forehead, but when I came close to her charm, something spoke in my ears. I was not able to make out what it was. As one confused by the lack of understanding of what was happening, I did not even believe in existence; everything seemed to me a dream. My grateful eyes and soul dwelt on that timid ray of light that gently caressed her smooth cheek, reflecting a wonder in my eyes and throughout our room, but you were nothing but a mirage.

In those moments, I felt that I had a divine friend whom I had never seen, so manifested as the next beauty and helped by the rays of the sun that spread like a holy spirit in the air to enter my mind as an invisible matter, a black hole that absorbed everything, above all, me, the first who carried the strangeness. An absurd soul enlightenment. My vision, which cleared every second, covered my beloved with an extreme beauty like an invisible laser beam; everything was invisible, even me. As for me, the sight of her gave me only love.

This mirage love reminds me of that tree that casts a shadow around its perimeter, does not allow any ray of light to penetrate under it; how heartless that tree is, neither happy nor happy, its life without light and only with shadow. It will remain gloomy for the rest of its life, how ironic, the hero tree. I opened and closed my eyes to understand what was happening, I was haunted in an empty and dizzying reality, but it was the same while her stunning beauty was beside me.

I was missing there, I was somewhere, but I didn't know where; I had lost myself and this terrifies me, maybe in my rigid imagination, but I could be happy. I wanted to go there but I didn't know how. I came out of my divine mirage and gazed upon that soulless curtain that barred most of those fantastic golden rays that came lazily. I rise with a merciless feeling. Out of boredom, I grabbed the object by force. I had lost my composure. I felt like I didn't belong in this world.

I lit a cigarette and started to inhale nicotine poison as if it were the only thing missing from that cast… but no, I hadn't instantly seen the happy city full of charm with people smiling so beautifully that the lazy light was ironic, and that was probably why she came without fun at my house.

At that moment, an original Parisian smile began to empty on my frozen lips, deforming my cheeks. As the sides of my eyes crinkled, I felt something I had forgotten. She was there in that bright room with the bottle of wine in her hand and two crystal glasses, anxiously waiting for me to go to her, or accept her arrival and confess my heart to you with the greatest confidence, dispelling the fear that he might not have to break it later by telling him something unusual. The smile, the key to love at first sight, and her presence made me stronger as my heart rate started to go crazy and she was coming straight to me, so slowly it seemed like it would never come. With her soft and rather fragile hand, like a child's, she lightly touched my hard shoulder. I began to tremble as my flesh turned to grain. At that moment, I felt like a small magnet absorbing great happiness.

For a moment, I leave the city surprised by existence and focus with all my being on her, on her sleepy eyes, which showed feeling and made her even more beautiful and clothed her with an exquisite feminine finesse. Her slightly wrinkled forehead expressed emotion, her half-open mouth expressed radiance, while her cheeks took on a flashy color that made me fall in love for the second time that day, but with the same beautiful feeling as the first time. The small oval beard gave an unscrupulous grace to the dignity of the charm she possessed.

With a soft hand on my shoulder, she frowned a little, straightened her forehead, lowered her eyes more, and with her beautiful mouth and chin moving slightly, she said to me, in a voice that I will never forget, "Dear, is love an epidemic?"

With tears in my heart, I saw that face that with every moment became more joyful. I raised my hand lightly, with great fear of hurting her with the roughness of my hard and lucky skin. I touched her face, I caressed every inch of her glowing, beautiful and soft cheeks that I felt the happiest person with the purest feeling, which emanated from the veins of the soul. With my numb black eyes going to every corner of her face, I didn't hesitate to answer at all.

"Humanity had no escape then."

She smiled – the third time I fell in love at first sight that same day. Apparently, she liked the answer, and it gave me a harsh feeling of kindness, but that smile took me into a world of adventure. My stomach started working. No no, I shouldn't have given you that answer, she shouldn't have exposed the shadow of laughter that he carried like a weapon and used whenever he saw coldness on my part. The deformation of the lips amazed me. I had never seen such a miracle before. I had seen it, but I had not known its value. I would like to talk more about love, that incurable disease, but more I wanted to row its pages, imagining myself in a boat of love, rowing in its calm waters. With those eyes under the eyebrows and black eyelashes, which gave an indescribable shadow, which served as a clear cloud to protect me from some nimble rays of the sun, he watched me for a long time.

To tell that I was the happiest person in the world was not lying at all, because I was, there was no one who was happier than me, many people can lie to themselves with lies and deception, but I would shut up if I told them what I had near and to what white shacks my mind took me, like a strange tourism where you couldn't take pictures. I would like to, but no, otherwise I wouldn't be the happiest person. My beautiful angel was being represented before me with her bodily charm, that body that anyone would fall in love with and desire at once to the point of drunkenness, while my eyes drop down, leaving for a few moments the wonderful image and smiling, radiating happiness. Her charming body clouded my thoughts so much that from the embarrassment of a strange feeling my hands sweated, my body seemed to be boiling, while at that moment my tongue tied senselessly because I imagined my little ship sailing on her cheeks fragile sank.

I didn't understand what happened. I wanted to say something, but at that moment I had no words, only thoughts. The situation started to become scary. I put my thoughts aside and cleaned my eyes. There was a window in the room, but it wasn't the one I had in my thoughts all the time. It didn't take long for me to learn that I had an extreme and ruthless imagination, but most of all I was alone in a world of dead ends, trying to make it as little as possible to get out into a world where reality had more sugar than imagination. I no longer trusted anyone, not myself, not the one who clinked the glasses against each other, not the favorite bottle of wine, nor the blazing fire, which burned and sacrificed itself with pleasure before me, testifying to a decoding of the new feeling of love which I did not had never been able to find out. That day everything had a mouth and a mind.

Only I didn't, so I closed my eyes to take a walk.

Reflection in Silence

I went to the bathroom and another person was reflected in the mirror. I didn't know him, it wasn't me, that's what I thought for a moment, because the only feature that caught my eye from that unknown face in the mirror was the reflection of misery. Surprisingly, it was me. This reflected in the mirror with my innocent appearance, I radiated not only misery, but also happiness. A frightening and sudden change. The mirror can only reflect an external view, but it never reflects your thoughts, those thoughts that both made me happy and made me feel very miserable. But very differently, this mirror knew how to do more than a reflection. I was happy because that divine beauty existed only in my imagination, and miserable because that same unprecedented beauty existed only in imaginations.

As I look at myself in the normalized mirror, inside I mourn, mourn for the kind of imagination that was driving me crazy. I had nothing more to do. Something inside me was telling me to give up, and I managed to read this in the reflection of the mocking mirror. Then I thought so, without imagination, to leave the toilet, that mirror that was not myself, because it reflected what it sees, not what it feels. I looked at her, full of anger, as I pretended to leave, as if the mirror were my enemy. I frowned, I gave her a knowing look of anger, so that she would take a threatening look from my side and fear me, putting a new order of authority. I clenched my fists so hard that my fingers started to crack and started to hurt. I wanted to hit her but very quickly I caught myself behaving strangely. The mirror this time reflected without speaking with her vital silence, so I didn't need anything else, just to tighten my lips and leave that strange room that made me hate an object, which was more normal, when I should hate the existence of my imagination that distorted my things, myself, reality, everything... that life with imaginations, it was driving me crazy. The bad thing was that I wasn't able to find what made me happy, while happiness is in imaginations, where I have the direction to do what I want, to put in people I loved and take out things I hated.

No. I didn't have access to invite Erin; she was an ice under my hot feet that was slowly melting. Pfff, I don't know what to do, keep my eyes closed and start thinking, or suffer from the ironic reality that lives under the cloak of imagination, which is separated by a thin membrane that can be broken by the echo of a very small voice? A groan. They are so close to each other that a blink of an eye makes the union. I didn't understand myself. I often imagine an event, remember it a second time and experience it the same way. Imagining Erina was a different feeling.

Probably a little bit of both. No, I do not agree with myself if I say madness, if I were to say love, feeling, affection, yes, I would quite agree, but although with some small doubts. On the contrary, I would agree with myself, with the imagination, the existence that all this was putting me in some unknown dead end where I didn't know how to get out. I see the light, but I'm not forgetting it, even though I've been walking this road for years, where my eyes are closed, but the sight is colorful enough. Images, miracles, illusions, nonsense, and all these things appear in the midst of the illuminating whiteness, that it surrounds every image of imaginative dreamy memories. Those memories that make you feel good when you experience them with your eyes closed, but make you feel bad exactly when they appear in reality as soon as you open your eyes. That reality that, with those beautiful memories and experience, could exterminate that bit of bitter reality that had invaded me with its invisible echo like a dive in the depths of the sea, but there was no sea.

The interior of that house was still lonely for me. Inside the house I still feel lonely. This feeling was driving me away from myself.

I think about this kind of crazy but real feeling. Loneliness is the tendency of intellectuality, and I said no to such an allusion in the mind, saying the opposite. Loneliness only terrifies me, even though it is beautiful at a certain time, a horror that I wish was imaginary, but no... it can't be, it's real. Sitting by the couch with my gaze fixed somewhere on an innocent object, embarrassing him unfairly, unintentionally, I go on and listen to my voice from inside the forehead, in that brain that apparently has those billions of cells only for thinking, not to get out of control, getting into an imagination so beautiful, so expressive, but also very exciting, making you sometimes confused whether you should love that genius of thought or hate him. My brain, along with surreality, has stopped some very vital and sensitive functions in the body.

The little lips that have forgotten to articulate a sentence, that have forgotten to feel another lip, that have thought and continue to think about their resurrection because they are dry from lack of water. Those lips were once very active, they were romantic and the most sensory organ in the body, these organs of dead cells and dried tissue have once kissed someone into existence, back when reality was the most beautiful routine I had. And here they are today, seemingly dead in reality. Due to their lack of attention, I had them on my face as an object of charm and attraction, but I had forgotten their value, because my body, soul, strength, words have been swallowed by an invisible force. Man is not afraid of the unseen, but of what he sees. They have faced the invisible, but apparently she has thrown a black cloak over her wings, so we do not recognize her as a danger. I manage to see that horrible object that deceives the wretched reality, but that frightens me beyond measure.

The Absurdity of Frozen Lips

I am free, but within me it seems as if I feel a suffocating spirit of imprisonment. Imagination has made movies, novels, even miracles; what it is doing to me is the embodiment of suffering and the extreme irritation of the irony factor of truth, which sends you unwillingly into a painful bewilderment. It's a beautiful thing to be between two worlds, but here it is and it's hard to experience that cruelly very satisfying feeling; it makes life difficult to the extent that you can manage to smile, that everything doesn't go any further.

In the imagination, within a surreal imagination, I beg the imagination, which has taken over my body and mind, to return me to the real world I know, not to this world where it itself makes you feel like you are acclimatized and then it seems impossible even to breathe. It seems to me that I am innocent, words that until yesterday I thought I knew the meaning of, but a voice that has conquered my soul, does not approve of this hint, tells me that I know too much and looks at me as if I had taken everything from that voice, dishonoring his potency. When someone is killed, only two people really cry at the funeral, the mother and the killer. If for some time and minutes I will not wet my lips with water, but not even a light kiss, I will have to sacrifice them in the name of imagination. I have to deny the existence of lips and see with regret their attitude, impresioned under the dark window of the mouth.

But where I was taking you, I didn't know. I'm very

confused. It's better for them to be where they are and be as they are. They have a few teeth from dryness and thirst. Don't add to the pain by giving them a definitive non-existent status; that would be funny in a funeral where you have to be in the position of the murderer.

A day will come, that someone useful will see them as organs that need saving and the need will arise to love them. Not knowing that they were creating an intermediary between life and existence, they would approach slowly, awakening the curiosity of crazy sensors from impatience that are in a long hibernation, and like a flower with her lips I will apply lightly and gently to life on the opportunistic lips for existing revival in the world of imagination and surreal reality, dressed with macabre indifference to mockery. After that, the fleshy and charming lips will no longer be dry, but full of life and ready to be constantly maintained. Who knows, that moment could be salvation for everyone. Until then, I have to be patient. I don't know how long I have to resist in this situation, but the records of the one who gave me life and existence and today directs our minds by disturbing and prospering us. I take a deep breath because my lungs had started the alarm. I wanted to enter more into this world of adventures where I can see and touch what I want without anyone imposing anything on me, except the beauty, which attracts you without words with its silence.

I want to drink, get drunk, why not go to the hospital, foaming at the mouth in agony until I no longer know where I am. I get up and with slow steps, with my legs dragging along with the desire to drink, I approach the minibar, that minibar, inside of which there is pleasure, desire, debauchery, but most importantly, inside there are two objects. Now I need them. It is the bottle with its characteristic shape with a thin mouth. I get closer to see something more. I clear my vision. I am surprised. I am speechless. No, nothing in that minibar was ordinary, just like my eyes darting here and there. My mouth closed and I felt like I was' coming down from a height fast, not surprised, as if this was ordinary; it wasn't. I realized what was happening to me. I started to accept this reality dressed in fantasy anyway, so, in confusion, I looked at the bottle which had the shape of a woman's lips, while the glass had the shape of a man's lips. An optical illusion too wonderful to be real and too deceptive to be fantasy. The minibar was so real that it was oval in shape, as if it could end somewhere, but I was not surprised but thoughtful.

I thought that the bottle didn't have the usual shape because, with its shape of lips painted with orange lipstick, like a virtuoso and exhibitionist, West would kiss the glass, that glass that had the shape of a man's lips. This lip shape looked very similar to my lips. I raise my right hand and lightly touch the bottom lip with my fingers, but I didn't leave a mark. It was fleshy, not hard like glass. It occurred to me that to replace the glass with the shape of the man's lips, the one with that rigid shape without tissue and with the sensor fallen into a lethargic sleep, with its equivalent, my lips, to play a little trick, was not bad. There was nothing wrong with that glass with the strange shape that made me kiss it. It was even a molded figure in the shape of an object, that glass that resembled its name; a more accurate name would be my lips. I didn't want to let that bottle kiss that accursed glass, but I said why not kiss my lips, this life-giving bottle shaped like a woman's lips so sought after that the first contact would give life to the cracked dryness of my organ, attractive and visible but lifeless?

That's what I'll do, I'll take the bottle and drink, kissing her lips like a mouth, and my lips like a glass. The moment I held that strange and vital bottle in my meat cup, I thought, if we have a problem and don't give it direction, we find the solution in alcohol – close our eyes, and we're where we want to be. When we open our eyes, we are not where we should be. I put aside the thoughts that drove me crazy and connected my lips to the bottle until I wanted to break it. At that moment something lighted up. A strong wind hit my face that almost froze me. My eyes closed for a moment from the air. My hair moved, as if it no longer belonged to me. Only when I felt that the storm was over did I open my eyes. What did I see? The room was darkened – at least from the point of view where I saw it, it seemed so. It was no longer those rays of light which reflected charm and love, but there was only one light which shined from above my head, just like that absorbing light of UFOs, but above my head I had no UFO, nothing. I had that glass that turned my lips back to normal, giving them the life I wanted, but not only that, the bottle had its own shape, that glass also had its own shape, just like an ordinary bottle and glass, so I thought I'd do a little trick, but it worked quite sweetly and beautifully for me.

Now I am happy because only I was not OK from all four sides of myself. Now everything was back to normal, except for me, because of this fairytale world I had entered. I thought it was over and I felt happy but also sad, because I still wanted to see strange unreal things, because I was tired of strange real things. I was wrong. With the bottle in one hand and the glass in the other, I began to fill it up to drink a big gulp until my throat stung and burned, tears welling up in my eyes and down my rough black-haired cheek. After drinking and drinking up to the limit of human metabolism, something happened to me. I did not separate the bottle from the glass, but only ruined myself even more by tiring my arms every time I filled the glass and turned it over.

The bottle was eased, the glass became heavy, my metabolism ate two thoughtless meatballs that a single mouthful was a painful dizziness. Then when the bottle went down to the mouth of the glass it was light. The ritual was heavy, lightness, drunkenness, ruin, debauchery.

The only sensation I felt in those moments was that I was losing my mind and a small pang of remorse for drinking. The world started spinning on my head. I started spinning around myself and everything around me. Everything was spinning around and around, breaking the balance of my thoughts so much that I held my head high for fear of falling somewhere, but it was useless; the drink was doing its thing. The beauty of all this suffering was that I was sitting still, and everything was spinning as if existence had forced it to exhaust me with its strings, making me feel like a half-dead idiot, but no, strangely enough the innocent imagination fueled by guilt was me, the imagination. I don't know if I'm guilty or innocent, I don't know if I should laugh at the burial of my reality or cry. One thing I know for sure: I didn't listen to what was happening and why my smile showed the hypocrisy that was sending a message to someone, and that someone did not exist.

Conversations with Lewd Fantasy

After the light of the dark contours of the dream was extinguished, and everything returned to normal, the darkness prevailed again. Fear was my best friend who smiled at me as if she wanted to flirt with me, but even this non-existence did not help me get through the situation where they lacked the need for real peace. The heartbeat increased, the veins stood out, my eyes reddened and at that moment I started a conversation with a stranger. In fact, I had seen him somewhere. We were both walking in a field of red roses in the middle of that frosty winter where the outside cold was absent, but only the inside, which had begun to freeze everything. I often glanced at the person in my arms who had no identity, to ask him for help or to ask him if he knew anything about my miserable and fearful situation. It was as black as darkness; it seemed as if it copied my movements precisely because this black shadow, which terrified me, was making my walking more difficult.

"Why are you following me?" I said, irritated, to that invisible thing. "Go away. I will go away where you are unknown, whoever you are."

"I'm not following you," the shadow politely returned to me. It gave you the feeling that it was smiling, but you couldn't see anything. "You go away to where you are known, because you entered my world, where you are the unknown."

"What is this?" I say to myself. "Am I not in a dream? If so, why isn't anyone waking me up to save me from this awkward feeling?"

"Surely yes," answers the shadow. "Don't wait for anyone to wake you up because you don't want help yourself. I saw it once. Everything I looked at, nothing seemed to be visible."

"What about the one where you hear me?" I got scared. Like a shell-less turtle in fear of eagles and their sharp talons, I wandered in the dark alone, vulnerable, slowly coming to terms with imaginary reality. What is happening to me? There were no more questions because the answer was obvious. Am I headed to Hell? There maybe...

"No, you won't go anywhere." A sweet female voice was heard. I turn my eyes from my eyes with the greatest surprise and fear of how he could hear the thoughts. She was in the distant time. My eyes went from the hand which I hold a watch, but it was invisible, I squint my eyes. I rub them hard until they start to tear me up and burn me. What do you see? The scorpions marked a time when it should be dark and it was because on the side of the bridge there was darkness, while on the other side a lightning, that was rushing... Wow, what a day. There, I realized that it is between two parallel worlds. Scary, if I had a choice.

"No," a sweet child's voice tells me. "It's not the light. You're dreaming and you're too much in the clutches of the imagination that has fixed your eyes so hard that you're not doing anything to escape. Just open your eyes, and you have your former life, but you've gone deep into fantasy and gone against it when you're not really yourself."

"I imagine, fantasize?" I wonder deep in my thoughts. I knew that everything I thought was heard.

"Maybe," she returns to me, "without going out, who is she?"

As soon as I looked further, a voice appeared to me. It was a sweet girl. Her green eyes were not real. She was several meters tall. Damn, it looked like me, but when I took a measurement I found out that I was half her size. I fell prey to an optical illusion.

"What's your name?" I ask her, however much I tried to take myself into submission and cause a spasm of revolution to shake my subconscious.

"I am your dream," the beauty returns to me. "Don't you feel me?"

"The dream?" I was surprised beyond measure and shook my head in denial.

"I am your dream, the unknown." The strangeness brings me back to a time when I was looking around for the child who had spoken to me, for the shadow that seemed to me like the reflection of my soul and a hell of a lot of things that I had encountered on the way. I gave a shout to use as a weapon in the hope that I wouldn't wake up, but the shout made several white crows startle and flap their wings in a rush of fear to escape.

Like white, aren't those colors... no, the world I'm in... the more I thought about where I was, the more I didn't notice where I was, I didn't understand anything, the more I lived with the absurd, but I was leaving the room and I was in a position to say with my subconscious mind that I am in a dream.

"Am I drunk? Perhaps, it can be so," I monologued to myself very unrelatedly when I knew how the situation was.

"No, you are not drunk." I hear another voice telling me. I felt that it was close to me, her breath told me that it was close to my ear, I had heard many voices until now, when I saw her... oh God, how beautiful she was, just like inspiration of nature for beauty... I was amazed, but it didn't allow me to fall in love with her. She was so beautiful, eyes with tails like Vietnamese, small lips like typical Asian, the only realistic beauty I was thinking.

But later, I realized that these are my voices in my mind that guide me in every solution. How much I had entered into myself?

"I didn't speak, I thought," I told him, and in the meantime, I sat down to shave my legs a little, because a huge and scary mosquito, which looked like it was going to swallow my whole blood with one suck, was drinking my blood, giving me the feeling that it was being I swelled.

"Here, I am the telepathy of people who do not know what is happening," he tells me. "We are your voices in your mind," he said again.

"What is telepathy?" I was surprised in record time. The next beauty was directed at me with a small mirror where I was completely reflected, as in murky water. I doubted if Narcissus would fall in love again in his life.

"Oh my God, what a monster…"

"It is not a monster and I deceived you that I am telepathy," the voice told me.

"Who are you?" I asked, scared and immediately showing fear and anxiety. My knees were cut until I no longer had the strength to stand. Everything in my body was shaking.

"Can't wait to introduce myself to you my dear." He turned to me and in his hand, he was holding a thousand-year-old parchment. She wanted to introduce me to me. Me with me, ironic, how funny.

"He-he-he, beautiful young lady who is in the form of voice, I know myself, I am imagination."

"I am fantasy." After he said this sentence, he made my mouth go numb because he froze me open. He extended his hand to finish this ritual of introduction. I was stunned; I was very afraid to touch him, even though it was like touching the air. I had not ever felt this kind of fear. I lowered my eyes and took a look at her hand. Her mouth was hanging open, her hand was… it was… strange, every finger turned and looked like a flower… I knew what to do, I held out my hand and when we touched I expected something soft, fragile, something iron, but no. Her hand was not like the hand I suspected. I realized this when the amazing fantasy withdrew her hand, leaving her fingers in mine, as soon as her eyes turned into roses, piercing my hand. I was not mistaken that they looked like flowers; they really were flowers. I had some blue roses in my hand. I was amazed at how beautiful that rose was, without thorns, but piercing. With raised shoulders, with hands raised in a sign of prayer, pointing humbly toward the Lord of the universe, I begged him not to give me any bad news. I could feel there was one and it was circling my head ready to hit me. The telepathy felt like it was me. When I thought about this I was happy, happiness that didn't last long because fantasy helps me.

"You, you are him," he tells me sweetly and frighteningly with a voice that begins to tremble at the end. I turned my head back, there was none.

"Who?" I returned it and my voice seemed to turn into an echo.

"He," he tells me.

"What are you saying? Fantasy beauty?"

"What you heard ugly imaginations. And that's where I introduced myself to you. Now you will know yourself better from now on. You will no longer have fluctuations."

"I mean, that monster that reflects my soul… is it me?"

She nods regretfully. "Turn your head, turn your imagination, dear, see yourself for what you are."

"See yourself?" As soon as I returned it, there were no mirrors to see how bad I had been, so much so that all of this seemed to me like a protest of my mind and interior, calling me to change. There were only a few people sitting with bottles in their hands, talking and trying to get drunk. I try to explain that under some narrow streets, there was a building with golden domes that radiated a light that split the sky into space. It was a mosque. But in vain.

"Come back, come back," she insists with her tempting and authoritative voice. I was a visible man in reality, that I had not known. I turned so slowly that it seemed to me that I had turned so gray that I had really turned into an invisible monster. The mirror was right, I was like Quasimodo.

"No, no, no," I cried instantly and felt a touch on my shoulder and a voice coming from far away, but I couldn't answer it, because I didn't like that my inside was presented by a mirror. "This, it's not me, it must be some optical illusion. Pull yourself together, pull yourself together. Ugh. I'm fine now. Oh, God, no."

I really became a monster, and I got revenge for all this absurd feeling. I turned into a bird and I don't know what. Am I not a fantasy in a wonderland? I turned my head from the fantasy, sad, frightened and with a young fringo spirit, with teeth sticking out of my mouth and hair.

Here was no one. Fantasy did not exist, same as existence. Metamorphosis, I thought. Oh no.

Scared and anxious, I turn my head from the mirror once more to see if there had been any change, because I swore that I would be good. There were those men who had already become jealous and were kissing each other out of the love they had for each other. Someone offered him a free drink when everything else was free, how ironic. I was scared, I was happy. The expression on my face changed. I looked funny. Courageously, I lowered my head to look at my feet. With one hand, I touched my back, which seemed to have some lumps in it, bending down to look at the horizon. There was no hump. I was no longer a monster, I was no longer the ugly children's character, like the Hunchback of Notre Dame, where everyone made fun of him but he knew how to love. While I didn't love myself, I really had the right ones, I was the imagination and that creature an optical illusion. To be the imagination of that winter's night with plots full of white roses, their petals covered with snow, was indeed the most beautiful image in all the dubious situations. My insides changed. I was who I was supposed to be. I was unchanged. The bad news was that this miracle of emotional swings was temporary.

Hand in Hand with the Dream, Through Pleasure

I was freed from the nightmare I thought I was in. I wanted something calm that was missing in those precise moments for idiotic thoughts. Everything was getting in my nose, everything was slandering me. Even my personal space was starting to disgust me. I wanted nothing, nothing. I opened and closed my eyes. It seemed as if I passed into another dimension of nature. I had to wake up several times because I was having too many dreams within dreams to make a little mess in the dirty neuron blur. The landscape was on a white side that didn't even give a damn about turning it red. It was snowing and there were rows upon rows of slandered daisies and tulips, their colors in harmony with each other but no impact on the spasms of thoughts almost beautiful enough to lie to themselves. It seemed to me like I was inside a Picasso landscape, but it was fake. From that landscape it is best built, but it lacks the only secret that Picasso often used in his works: to know how to paint a book within a picture. This is the nightmare of a painted landscape, patronized by people who want to destroy nature and express it according to their often dark mind. A bee stops at a purple flower to collect nectar to make honey and pollen to feed the queen they respect so much, not because they love her but because they fear her. A squirrel playing with some blades of grass appeared, who had lost his delicious hazel but had found an alternative game to lose his small and narrow mind. A bunny eating a carrot moved its mouth and whiskers at supersonic speed, a patch of juicy dates, some vines with grapes, a waterfall humming like the sound of a shell when you put it in your ears after we pulled it out of an ocean and a silent writer at the end.

I was astonished at last to see one whom I recognized as a species, but when I met him, he muttered something to me and went away.

"The bad and the good are separated by a thin transparent thread," he told me in a muffled voice, wearing a look of disgust on his face, as if he was stuck somewhere. "The good thing is to have a writer as a friend, it's bad to have a writer as a friend. Their world is so vast that they masterfully manage to reduce your world to the point where you either call it stupid, or you become the stupid one."

The colors gave me a golden feeling in my soul. Beyond was a hill that seemed to have mouths and eyes. Its bleak and dark appearance terrified you, but the hill looked at the people with cares. This beautiful panorama was disturbed only by a voice coming from below. It was the voice of the writer who told me to wake up, wake up, wake up Erin and the trunk. I ignored it. He had no hands, no voice, no eyes. There was just a hint of white from the snow. The top of the trees were covered with snow. This appearance in interaction with nature, gave an optical illusion like a white shirt. This hill with its charm, whitch shone with whiteness, people still saw with hatred, with fear, as the place of the different stories.

This is the small irony of humanity, that we recognize a giant object as invincible, until we have nothing else to do, until we hate it. Small minds hate, big minds lie. This beautiful and small hill looks like an orphan, like the shadow of a mountain, where years ago a solid line of liquid fire cut through it, but I also thickened it by describing a great path from the interior of the Earth, lava and magma made plans about how many people they would kill, how many houses they would destroy, how many rivers they would dry up, that is, how much damage they would do. The mountain listens to the pathetic humiliation of two cruel and heartless friends and decided not to break, resisting to the point of sacrificing itself until I cause an avalanche and the top decided that mountain will be unopened.

This great mountain was the unwitting victim of evil goodness, evil that was given the name goodness, and the two together formed a savage tragedy where it would destroy innocent victims once, to forever protect other generations. For years, that mountain was never understood, forced to be the lustful sight for the hatred of the people who despised it when it most needed a little glory, then forced for days to emit convictions while inside, the womb of the beast put up a flaming war of resistance. The mountain, the father of this hill, who loved so much the inhabitants of the city where it lay, and who looked down upon them because they had never understood his goodness, was shaken with rage to warn them of some disaster, that they should leave as soon as possible. Their fear increased, and so did their hatred. The mountain sadly saw his people despise him for the last time in his agony of surrender, saw not only his beauty and majesty with those gray hairs, benevolent, but also the news he brings where it was never understood by the inhabitants. He was then forced to break. The mountain succumbed to the two friends after many, many fights within it, the snow fell like tears on its steep slopes, the peak began to wear out, from within it had been fighting for a long time, the anger was great, so in a hurry a volcano erupted which was red, black, orange, it was multicolored. His lava completely melted his hair, replacing it with colorful, cruel lava.

The inflamed sea slid under his stature with stubbornness, depicting the drunken city and all the disobedient inhabitants of the good and the bad, who plunged but never came out of hell where even Paradise could not save them. Therefore, this innocent little hillbilly enjoyed the bad reputation of her father. A butterfly passes very close to my nose. It joined several other butterflies with golden wings, with dots like ink balls where it seemed as if this beautiful landscape was made by a painter dipping his pen into the ink balls of this butterfly. Another had wings like the color of the Norwegian west. It pleased the eye as you sat there and watched that group of friends bring them round and round, around a playground, then, waving their arms and smiling in my face, they came straight to a river where, as soon as you looked at this river, you saw a miracle that you had never seen before, a rainbow of colors, colors where Picasso would come to gain experience and knowledge, and again he would have great difficulty in expressing all his emotions in a picture of only abstract, because everything was perfect.

The river of pleasure, that's what the stream was called, meandered through the city of dreams where some children made miniature boats out of paper and set them afloat. Pleasure did not wet their boats for the happy and harmonious little girls, but made fun of them by holding them on the surface to float even a little calm enough to get a small dose of happiness. It made it behave just like a playful river. It was a true paradise that I would really like to live in a place where there was no crime, no accidents, soothing greenery enlivened, green everywhere, all kinds and so many colors with flower plots. The green river was unusual in that it had living things that floated on the surface so as to avoid the miniature paper boats made with a lot of creativity of the children taking care. Their scales were changing. I don't know what to say; I was in the imaginative world of dreams and all this I didn't want to be a dream, a painting. They were nymphs. I was confused.

Dark Feelings

I opened my eyes. I saw darkness. It seemed to me that I had betrayed myself, I had sold my heart for charity, and my soul looked at me with astonishment at my actions. With a frozen heart, I looked around in horror. I felt that I was water in sweat, I was in existence, what about me in the beautiful body of reality? In her trick? No, I don't want it; I don't even want inspiration, I don't want reality, I don't want anything, just to close my eyes and seriously be imagination. My heart was pounding, my veins had turned from green to red, my eyes hurt. I felt swollen; my breathing was fast and the place where I had rested my head was stained with sweat mixed with hair gel. I started to scratch my head and looked at the TV. It slanders me, the same things here in reality. I wanted to steal. I didn't want the dirt of the routine, but what did I do, I was in the palliative world of things where you can't change the end, but they only pushed it. I felt that I was dirty, dusty, my soul was disgusted by those deceptions that everyone says on television. I turned off the TV I had bought because I had to have one. I walked and with difficulty – I limped a couple of meters because my leg was numb – I took a glass of wine, the bottle of red Chardonnay, and filled it halfway and started drink it to the sounds of French music. I excited the throne of the glass by inserting my fingers, intertwined with my fingers a wave of melody, squeezing it hard to make her moan, to feel her body. I expected from moment to moment that the throne would break from the lust to drink, but my fingers were also not strong on the scales, causing my hand to tremble, which caused vibrations inside the glass. The fingers were inserted between the shaft that holds the oval shape. I lifted it slowly. I brought it to my nose; I smelled it. After smelling it I turned it, I turned it until I completely lost my mind. The wine ran from one side to the other. My eyes were on the rippling shapes forming in the glass, giving it a pale red color of excitement and desire.

In the depth of the wine glass, it had taken on the dark color as if it were blood without oxygen. I was completely hypnotized. I didn't know how to get out of this senseless project of my deluded brain. It was very similar to a psychological sleep. Do you mean it to be so? With the clouded thought in my head, I went out to my balcony that I had; the only reason why the rent was so expensive was because I could see the Eiffel tower, when in fact the house served for nothing but as a hotel to drink this glass of wine. I wanted to drink it in solidarity and harmony with time, with the chirping of the birds that formed a symphony, with the rustling of the leaves of the trees, which seemed like a jet plane passing at supersonic speed, but no, those rustlings caused a slight puff of wind. High in the sky was a plane that shot plumes of smoke, chemical or not. The people are out of the game in this kind of news. I once shook the wine by thundering so hard that it made a terrible groaning noise, but it was nothing like her. I shook my head slightly and smiled. I opened the balcony door more and there was a hateful noise. I closed the door quickly. Silence fell, only my breathing and a few hard thuds coming from inside the chest could be heard. Boom-boom, boom-boom, bang-quiet, bang-quiet. It was still lunch.

Rested in my stillness, sheltered from existence, and guarded from the cries for survival from the outside world, my mind rested somewhere, not far away. Stick to it, my heart is tired by sending alarm signals to the brain, the brain tells the stomach, "Give that feeling of lovers and say that you are being deceived," because the sky of Paris has never been so symbolic of sincerity, it is still a figment of the imagination. I felt a huge knot in my stomach and stress cortisol coursing through my veins. It didn't hurt, but I was shivering like a dog in the cold. The only thing missing was the expression of the request for help with my eyes, enough to look miserable, otherwise I won't hurt anyone. I had to squeeze into the vibration that helps me get rid of a loud noise, an echo, so I did, I clenched my hands tightly, rested them firmly on my stomach and squeezed, letting out a cracking noise where I finally failed. Unable to talk, I thought, with the glass in my hand, that I still hadn't finished.

"It will be a dream if she goes out with me tonight… I don't know if he read that message on his phone five minutes ago, by the way, where is my phone? That dream didn't do me any good, it seemed to me, it swallowed me up as if I were a river that takes everything forward and mercilessly, throws them down in a waterfall to destroy everything, from feelings to life itself. Inside a river where you have no livelihood, life seems like nothing."

I picked up the phone. I saw that he hadn't sent me anything, at least a message, but no, nothing. He was heartless, I thought, and for a moment I hated him. It's so easy to hate someone, just think bad about them and it only takes a second.

"The man sends a message, out of courtesy." I started to get angry at you, unintentionally. If she doesn't want to go out, she just doesn't want to go out, period. I would spin the phone with stress like a spinner that would not stop spinning, sometimes killing my fingers from the stress because the waiting was causing damage to my nervous system. Suddenly, I felt that someone felt sorry for me, for my nervous health.

It was the cortisol hormone that thins out its large flows, I don't know, but a wave of optimism overwhelms me again. In these moments, as a sign of satisfaction, I closed my eyes. Oh, how calm I felt, as if she... I said it, full stop. I didn't care if he didn't accept it, but the hypocrisy of someone looking for an answer is that there is no one to expect one from. This is where the lie wins, befriending a dark feeling to overcome your imaginary loneliness. At least for a few seconds, you feel that it is a feeling you forgot to feel. A voice called me, a knock, as if I hit the wall, brought me back to normal. That voice was hers, but on my phone, and what was calling was the darkness. Silently, I realized that I was the only prisoner of my imagination and I was so deeply involved that the real world was confused and I didn't know when to leave.

Lying Fantasy

Two things you cannot buy after you have sold them: masculinity for men and honesty for women. While I was waiting for the message from the lady I had recognized on the white lines of the pedestrians, I hear a dirty thud that appears in my mind as something bad that I had to respond to so that it doesn't happen again or doesn't last long.

"What is it?" I asked the silence. I turned my eyes in surprise. She shrugged. I was the curiosity in this orgy of meaningless roles. I opened it to read. I immediately took it to the end to see who had sent it to me, because the rest was in the background, because the first plan was to see the last words, to hear the subject of the message. I wasn't finding the courage to be a little spontaneous. At the end was her name; that's what I wanted. I was happy when I saw something like that and with happiness on my lips, I started to read it with a slowness like the erosion of the wind, so much that I started to get tired, as if I had read a thousand paintings for hours. She wrote:

That unpaved road, with potholes everywhere and puddles everywhere, in the middle of the white lines with a view of the Eiffel, where you were holding your head up to see the top and we were bumping into each other's shoulders, in the area where drivers should increase the intuition of caution to pedestrians, see you. They loved that watering hole and that special moment to get to know you under the guise of absurd circumstances, but not only that, they also loved that charming and energetic and slightly myopic retired old man who had no mercy for me, the lonely lonely pedestrian splashing me. What we want, and it is not too difficult to achieve, is to give us a little more priority. No, the account is a disaster. How well you did, grandma, that you sprayed me. You were selfish by calling everything yours; thank you for not being in the effect of altruism. You would be a sinner with a certificate of shame... if you paid attention to me and my priority, you would not be here today a special one, but ordinary. I saw that you were amazed. I noticed in your eyes how you saw me. In those moments, I must admit that I was amazed in front of you. Two brains, one thought, two hearts, one love, Tolstoy said, isn't that beautiful? I felt like a princess when you were next to me. You politely offered to clean my pants made of mush by selfish myopia... nothing saved my pants from water, but you did yours with the intention of entering a little chat with me. Your smooth cloth gave me pleasure, my body tingled and I started to get excited. I wasn't cold, but my flesh was tingly. You apparently stood there, ready with your rag to catch the next deer. I don't know how old you were there, but I looked like Robin Hood. The rain had stopped, the sky had cleared and with an amazing blueness, the sun was sending some strong, flattering rays, as if to say, enjoy these rays because I'm going away again, you took off your gold-rimmed glasses, green mirror. I saw myself in those two ovoid circles, but in an instant you looked like those princes who dismount from the white horse with a sword. You didn't have a horse, you had glasses. You didn't have a sword, you had a cloth. How the stories of dolls have changed! Go out with you? Why not? What harm would you do to me if I tried drinking a glass of wine in a romantic setting with light piano music? A Mozart, a Beethoven, and some paintings made especially for this moment? It will come out, but on one condition, that you tie my shoes for a month in a row. Good? The doe who suddenly turned into a princess, who suddenly met the prince in the white lines of the pedestrians, turned into porridge. Could this be a divine message? Wait until I think of something. Hmmmm... wait, hmmm... a little more, hmmm. I don't agree to go out with you. You are kind of heartless; you look how you look, you steal girls' hearts and with them you can make a soup that you can mention a name in every spoonful you lift. Bad, you are bad. But you are also good. Where are we going to meet? Finally, these signs and this coincidence indicate something. I say let's find out. Don't we leave the house tricked with chemicals that we know are bad for us to look good. That day I didn't make someone for myself with my trick, but with simplicity.

I took a deep breath, the air hissing in my nose, and my chest heaved and heaved from my lungs so full of air that they seemed to burst. Everything didn't seem like a message, it didn't seem like a reality, it didn't seem like a dream. I closed my eyes, happy and smiling, still holding the glass of wine in my hand with my fingers interlaced on her throne, standing in a strange synchronicity, with half of my mind connected to not being completely disconnected from the cold reality. I started to turn it again. I was glad because in the darkness that appeared when I closed my eyes, I saw someone running toward me, a great desire to kiss him with lips that melted a glass in the shape of a lip, from thirst for them stuck with kisses, a wave of excitement went through me until I felt a bit of a sting as if to reprimand my feelings. Her barren black hair that seemed to hold an undisclosed secret, her small olive eyes that expressed everything to her cruel beauty, her soul is as beautiful as it is in the sparkle of her eyes. The eyes looks bright, when in really she lacks the brightness of herself.

The forehead, even and harmonious in the mystery hair, and with merciless, unwrinkled eyes, there was only a straight line as if someone had made it by hand, in the form of art until I thought that it could not be an earthly one, and not even a chance that came from nothing turning us into monkeys. It was clear when you saw Erina that we are God's masterpiece. To talk about her lips painted with closed red lipstick, shapes that you would be sorry to kiss, so as not to spoil the shape, the beautiful image that they had which was flawlessly graceful and with an unprecedented attitude, sometimes and never painted, let me then contemplate the pale cheeks with a little light lemon powder that seemed to reflect her charm in full wonder, portraits that have not even been seen in Picasso's most famous paintings. Mona Lisa began to smile, giving meaning to the world. The smile moved the ears a little, creating a dimple in the corner of the cheek, where the cheeks melt their beauty into the smile and show through the eyes that a soul exists, even so special that we know nothing about it.

Everything was perfect, I couldn't wait for him to come to me, touch him and feel like the happiest and luckiest person in the world. When he approached me, he lightly touched my cheeks with the back of his hand, not as I had imagined because nothing we imagine comes true. To fly? I didn't know… to love him? I couldn't… feel it? I didn't dare… but why? Because I feel inferior to the beauty she has, as much as my beauty I reproach the charm for her bad luck, but even so I was not so bad. Her beauty was intimidating, her touch thrilling, causing her hand to caress my cheeks like a lazy cat purring in pleasure. Grrrrr-grrrrr, grrrrrrr-grrrrr. Hell, I opened my eyes. I was in an extra-human and inter-worldly dimension never seen before. I had fallen asleep. There was no cat around, but me snoring with my head resting on an arm rest of the couch. Because I was sitting down on a cushion, my throat was tight, so I started snoring louder than usual. How I wish I was a macho, but to stay in that dimension, not in this mess, where the wonder was too chronic, there was nothing apathetic about that world, when it came to beauty, the art of seduction. The return was the awakening within the dream. Someone pretended to touch me in the soup and call me, while I listened to him like a dead man who wants to come back but can't. His trial in this world is over.

I had lost track of the clock and time. I saw the glass of wine that was there as I had dreamed and I smiled. I saw the plate of dried fruit that was empty and then I closed my eyes once more, hoping to return to him once more, the absurd reality that, damn it, was fantastic.

Love with Space

I lived a hermit's life. I lived alone, I ate alone, I slept alone, I drank my glass of wine alone, and the only friends I had were those imaginary ones, that writer who was looking for escape routes and some bees. Society had abandoned me because I wasn't realistic in the life they led. I always told them about the mistakes and they returned to me arrogantly, that's all you need. Stay and see those good friends, who did not pay attention to me at all, and even described me as a person who came from an external world and who lived in a pragmatic dimension in my internal world. So that one winter night when I was bored was my final departure from their circle where I did not once understand them or me, and the moment when I dreamed about the impossible with my eyes open and closed. What does this matter? They didn't want people like me, they wanted adventurous types, who drank alcohol from morning until dinner and were debauched with their exploits. I lived alone for a long time because when I was with my prejudiced friends, when I was with all my prejudiced friends, all I heard was, how did Eiffel build the famous tower, or why don't I build it two meters further and a series of idiotic theories.

They all pointed the finger at me with one voice and told me to go away. I didn't have a car, so I decided to do those tens of kilometers on foot, because no one moved, at least to drop me on a piece of road. I was bored with my friends, I was bored with myself, I was bored with our galaxy, with the universe, with people, with everything. After two hours, I arrived home. I was exhausted. As soon as I entered the house, I remembered my ex-girlfriend that I loved so much that this love passes into disrespect on her part. It reminded me of how she used to wait for me at home, with the lights off, creating a romantic atmosphere that only the French know how to do, at least one thing they knew how to do well.

It was a pleasant surprise when the soul said to me, "Is love a disease?"

I smiled at her. The night looked white; the moon smiled at me, the stars formed a tableau where the twilight darkness of the stratosphere served as a blackboard to write the universe her way. They wrote: kiss, caress, she needs a hug, don't shed tears, and such things. It was the night when we made love until dawn, but it was also the last time we were sensitively touched, because a glass wall separated us. During the evening, I had opened the curtain a little to see the Eiffel tower, allowing the playful moonlight to enter our souls and we reflected it in the room like a great love in the middle of the darkness. The wine glasses were half full, where during the act, everything rested only for a precious sip of wine. When I wake up in the morning, she wasn't there. That was the last time I saw her, because she ran away from me for no reason and the cynics' words were that I hadn't satisfied her enough in bed, even though I know she reached her orgasm over four times, one time after another. She imagines when you feel that you had gone four times more in the sky. Or had I lied to her about my romantic imagination when you told her about what the stars said?

This night remained a mystery. Above all, we, from that night we parted. I would walk down the street to some promenade, buy a drink and drink until morning, just because none of my friends understood me, or I didn't understand them, or they didn't know what they wanted and I had found what I wanted, opening the door of confusion to them. My friends together with my friends despised me as soon as I passed by them. I loved them. Once this happened, after that I always went away from them. I was forced to do this, because I could not hear their voices that were like thunder with sparks. I knew that they hated me for no good reason, so in order not to hurt their hearts more, I tried to avoid them. But even they couldn't stand me, that's what they said to turn the situation in their favor because the truth was that they didn't understand me. Once, when I was running home, I ran into him, which bed and imagination separated us.

She does not accept my invitation to make love with sensitive touch, with soothing words and with looks where the oasis of prestige of feelings is not finished. Perfection could be a wild fantasy, but here it was a forbidden affection in a world without laws. She could not hold this thing, this great mirage of feelings in her suppressed soul and filled with all kinds of dangers and filth; she was too small to cope with such great feelings and to know how to make selections. Even the moon scared him, the purple sunset made him feel traumatized, while nature with its calmness whispered in his ear beautiful things, full of colors, organized enough for the unbearable soul of a person who has no way to keep even two joys in the soul filled with bitterness, the heart beating hard from the heaviness, making life a myth, an undeserved adrenaline, that made you walk on the white road, with eyes wrinkled and blackened from filling the soul with things bad. As soon as you enter the worlds you fought to enter, you face a war with yourself that you have lost. Yet, without entering into that self-understanding, she does not accept the feeling, even though they are so beautiful, but also so meaninglessness. In the end, we are afraid of it, of the beautiful. I don't know what happened, but that night I got a message; she didn't love me for what I was, but for what I should have been.

I gestured to her to give her a chance to be with me so that she could be cleansed of the dirty residue in her soul, but she didn't react. I spoke, but again she ignored me. In those moments, I found myself more empty in this sphere full of propaganda about the good that bad people do. With wounds in my soul and a broken heart, I started on my way to my house, where a comfortable armchair and a good wine were waiting for me, with which I would spend the whole night until the sun came up. I spent many nights waking up, having orgies with the moon, sometimes with the sun in the presence of the glass of wine that was a fearful open mind, sometimes forgotten by attention even though empty. It carried an aroma of reckless love with no other feeling that gives you the thrill of smell. What can you do in one lifetime when you have so many things to do? Nothing, that's why people accept defeat, because failure is stamped on their minds. My bed was no longer filled by anyone, not even the sun with its rays that consumed my space every time. It was not me because it burned me. It did not know how to make love without damage. I could not even resist the moon, because it surrounded me and penetrated me in a whirlwind of darkness where I could not see anything, and it caused many tides in my soul. I tossed and turned through the night, but still ended up in that chair with a view of the stars, bottle of wine in hand and my best friend, the ironic Eiffel, and the bitter taste of the drink along with the dizziness.

When I met the stranger at the white lines, it had rained all night and why was she so infatuated with me? I never wanted her to enter my life. I knew she would leave immediately, traumatized. And what was I? The most vain man in the world. I gave her the number, and to avoid asking her to go out, I was already afraid of every ring, lest she tell me that we are going out. That's why I often imagined that she might do this pleasant but undesirable thing. She seemed to be a lively, beautiful girl, while I was a loner, sitting alone like a mute with no one to talk to, despite the fact that I had a mouth and a voice. Everyone hated these favors. Anyway, when I went home after that chance meeting, I did the same things, only this time I was very imaginative. This happened to me by myself. This was the moment I imagined her with her soft hand gently touching my lips, blocking the sunlight, everything. In these critical moments, in the name of imagination, I gave myself up. So, I created my imaginary friends, who didn't despise me but loved me. How good I feel when they love me. Be it imagination or reality. I suddenly started to feel a heaviness in my lap, while lips were touched by other lips that came with a distant voice, a familiar voice. I couldn't move, I couldn't do anything. I knew I was dreaming, and at the same time I was possessed by that world.

I Want to Curse Myself by Drinking

The greatest greed of the imagination is to surpass it, to lose, to be fascinated, to be excited but not to reach any satisfaction, and in the end to be left with a shore. How could it not be true? In the room, as always, I was suffocated by loneliness, pressure and apathy. I couldn't even stand the TV, so I had put it to sleep with the depressive remote control of my sick mind in the last steps. The glass of wine seemed to reprimand me for neglect by looking down at me, but could do nothing more. A faint ray of sunlight struck the lifeless chest of the TV and then into my eyes like a menacing swirl. I was mesmerized by the supernatural beauty. Everything seemed amazing to me, even a fluorescent pony with pink hair who was silent, but knew how to make a lot of noise to attract attention. You don't need noise to attract attention.

I eclipsed the beam of light as I faced the television, the light falling on my chest like a veil draped in a magic cloak to give me supernatural powers of thought, not action. Already I fell in love with the natural phenomena, the curtain reddened by the setting sun drenching everything with its charm. I closed it by attaching both arms with a clothespin to be as strict as possible with its rays, taking the shape cast from above with the heart space upside down, just like in Shakespeare's tragic scenes. The light entered a strained form within, as if it were its own purpose. I pulled back, walking backwards. The curtain took on an orange color, where it seemed to me like a magic scepter that had turned my house into an imaginary kaleidoscope. This color was reflected in the whole room, as well as my body as a paler shade. With the color stimulated, with the glass in my hand, the miracle did not take shape... Something was missing. I thought long and hard to solve this problem that for no one was like that. For me, yes. I raised my hand, took out a big glass of wine as soon as I could. When I put the glass down it was much easier.

I started to pass it through the palate, spreading through the teeth, the inside of the cheeks, taking my eyes from left to right. My mouth got a sour and bitter taste, a special taste that started to close my eyes and my lips wrinkled a little. Then he remembered something. Somewhere in the room, I had some rose petals and some colorful indie-scented candles, which I kept when I made love to Erina, my ex-girlfriend who ran away, left me because she wanted a sleepy love in my silent bed. Don't judge her, please; this is how she agreed to act. It's her opinion and in honor and grace of the love I have and have had, I have to respect the decision. It's a wool decision, but that's what I have to do. The world on Earth calls this courtesy and respect. The imaginary world that I am, desire and freedom. I went to look, left behind the red scenery in the kitchen and hurried to my room, which was a disaster every time I thought about going there. On the way, I thought, what if they are not?

Lost in a whirlwind of thoughts, I walked nowhere, bumped into the door rail, turned around and glared at him so much that I almost cursed him, then just before I said sorry, I shook my head and left him behind the door, along with my idiotic thoughts. Open a drawer, nothing... open another, again empty... another, still nothing... a wave of disappointment began to overwhelm me. I was sad, I had nothing to do. I gave up, shoulders slumped, with my arms swinging like a pendulum. I left the room of disappointments. All the hope of my beauty, the thirst for wonder, the desire for the wonderful, remained in that fluorescent pony who seemed to me to smile at every disappointment and by this, he meant that I am here, but you forgot to appreciate me. I took it in my hand; it seemed as if it laughed. I laughed too. It's good that I was alone because I was acting very strange, I was imposing on myself the world of illusion, the power of prestige, the beauty of imagination.

    I left the pony, took lighters, matches, some wooden cylinders and started to light the fireplace. That fireplace that I lit every time Erina and I made love, surrounded by scented candles that I missed. Maybe they could have finished. The flame of the warm fireplace seemed virtual. I rejected this illusionistic and prestigious imagination because I could feel the flame burning my face. With the help of nature for beauty, with the inspiration of love, with unimaginable illusions, and with soulless abandoners, I created a miracle myself, a miracle that even an unnatural being would immediately fall in love, not with me, but with the environment, with the colors blazing, with the fire resembling the wings of a butterfly, full of lovers' names on the wings. Imagination or reality, I was able to share this experience, not just me, but with billions of my fellow travelers. We are all on a train that fate has determined for us, several stations. Knowledge is in our hand, in our destiny, in our intuition. A good acquaintance, mercilessly we call love.

*

Still no answer on the phone. This terrified me, disturbed my thoughts until I was silent in myself, enough to call it closure in itself. It is better to be hurt by the truth than to be comforted by lies. I didn't know what I was doing. I was a mess. Oh God, I'm starting to love my imagination more than my Erin. I love everything that happens there. Just close your eyes and do whatever you want. You can see geese in the Himalayas, you can see tigers swimming in an air pool in northern Tibet, crocodiles that walk people in the city, sharks that take pity on life and ignore the smell of blood even though they are very hungry, vegetarian eagles, see themselves with Erina, but immediately feel sad, fall in love with her directly again for the umpteenth time, leave everything for well. In the end, it is me who chooses what to do. I choose the best, the worst because I know it doesn't hurt me, it only strengthens me. I choose whether Erina will return, or whether the unknown will bring me a message or not, I love, above all, the imagination that makes me see things where I can't, no one sees you.

I love imagination and I want to live in dreams. I scare people with my absence, with my isolation, with all-round realism, I make them feel agnostic until they think about why I exist. The setting was romantic at a time when I was very romantic, why me? Am I not in love? And with whom? I don't know… I've been in the world of dreams. In reality, not all answers are given to the questions that are asked. I have the answer to some, but I don't want to do it… let me comfortably drink another glass of wine, too, then swallow me up like a waterfall that looks like a white bridal veil, which as you throw it, become a body, causing a watery erosion toward the softness, the foam, and the calm coldness there at the bottom of the sea, at the beginning of natural freshness. Please let me laugh at myself because no matter how much I live and think about the reality of fake people, I love them more because they stay away from me. Voluntarily.

By the Suicidal Chimney

I don't want to be separated from the environment where I am, but I have to admit that I am in the hated reality, where everyone pretends to be what they are, everyone gives reasons to hate it, or to love it, why not to be deceived? Glass in hand, I sit by the fireplace. The flames seem to break from the top and disappear enough to fixate. The best carved stones give this flame and this environment an indescribable, sublime and very satisfying feeling, but above all strange, as if living in the ancient time of hieroglyphs. The heart doesn't feel; are you saying it's not there, are you saying it's in agony? Even the desert one is in a rut. I don't know what to do, to cease to exist or to continue her tedious work. For a few moments, I forgot about the candles, I forgot about her messages, I wasn't expecting anything anymore. Sitting on the ground, on top of a blue cotton pillow, with the darkness abounding and the light scarce, I felt something. It was a phone ring. I regretted this call, as much as I was enjoying that solitary reality at that moment. I was annoyed because I loved the already hated selfishness so much. I don't know why after that bell I started to spin the glass with the straws, the wine spread everywhere in the glass, coating it with a crimson color. The edges of the wine looked like mountains and like sea waves. I was thinking that I love reality and hate imagination when I'm here. But I love imagination when I'm there and hate reality when I'm not. I said these things in my imagination, then I emphasized out loud, as if the fire had contradicted me about something that

I was right about. I was leaving as a philosopher, where I had my argument and I was always right; after all, this is philosophy.

Explain the absurdity in a few words so that not everyone can understand it.

"Yes, yes, I love reality." And I was nervously pointing my finger at the fire. Another piece of fire broke from the top and disappeared straight into an unknown world. The fractal shapes of the fire grew heavier and heavier, making him crave wood. I still hadn't opened the message. I was afraid, I don't know why. It could be Erina apologizing to me, it could be the unknown lines of the road telling me to get out. I never found the courage for something so basic. I feel like I've given up on everything. Fear appeared in reality, anxiety in imagination. I closed my eyes and began to imagine. I don't know why, but the imagination immediately made me open my eyes quickly from the anxiety I experienced instantly.

"Why, imagination? I love you," I thought and raised my shoulders. But no one answered. I went, I frantically went somewhere to find the phone. I leaned a little to the left and to the right as if my house was on the sea, and damn, at that moment there were a lot of waves. I was going in the wrong direction; the phone was somewhere back where I came from. The wine in the head was what put the right side of the brain into conflict with the left side, creating a Big Bang of thoughts. The result was I found myself moving without knowing where I was going and what I was looking for. From a few meters away, my eye caught an object that still had the light on; this caught my attention. Then the light went out, leaving the find to the mercy of my intuition. It was dark everywhere; the fire in the fireplace was capitulating, the sun was no longer brilliant that on the front of my balcony it gave the curtains that dark color. This dark object began to like me, there was no need to close my eyes to imagine. For them, I comforted myself with lies, but I stared somewhere where the light didn't beat. From there, I could imagine with my eyes open, at least be hurt by the truth. Thinking, I approach the place where the gossiper's phone was, with my eyes open, but unable to see. I began to search with my hands, trying to see by touch. I touched the precious phone that scared me. I had left it on the headboard. My hands were shaking, a wave of nervousness engulfed me, my right eye was throbbing. I took a deep breath, this time as hard as if it was the last time I would put oxygen into my lungs. My lungs lied at first, but then, the saturation is not missing. I picked up the phone with unsteady hands. There was an unread message written on the front screen. Is it unknown? What if Erina tells me... I have to find out. I nodded with a faint smile, as if someone was forcing me to. I opened the message, I was disappointed.

Existence, are you up for a beer? Reality.

This ironic fellow wanted to drink beer with me. Isn't he left alone like me? They don't even understand reality anymore? But I do not fall on the neck of others with irony and sarcasm like that. I just thought. I pursed my lips in annoyance. I didn't expect that, I'm in the imaginary world anyway and this is where... the unexpected happens. I thought I would return the message with the same sarcastic irony, something for many. These are the people, with irony and sarcasm pretending to frighten the enemies, not knowing that no one is frightened by the wealth of your knowledge. But I knew that it would disturb my peace. I didn't know what to do, confusion took over me. Her wealth of knowledge had come into conflict with my wealth of patience. I let go of the glass of wine, the self-extinguishing fire, the light crackling of the embers, the beige and brown stones around, the hieroglyphs, where a ship tilted with sails, high mast, and slavish laborers were carved on the wall. On the other hand was a prehistoric bird with an olive crown like the Greeks. The fluorescent pony from the darkness seemed to hover in the air. All these confusions are hurting me. I feel like I'm getting gray. I need all the strength to have the courage to make a decision, which I lacked in those moments. Life was a struggle for survival. Yes, I liked drinking a beer while walking on the city boulevard with the noise of cars and people coming straight, ready to fall on the shoulder, but I didn't like the person I was going to be with. I like the environment where I am, the calmness, the solitude, summer, fire. It seemed to me as if I was in a world surrounded by gods. I was actually alone. I go once more near the window. I removed the clip that held the two sides of the curtain and a wave of light hit me. I hastily put my hand to my eyes, creating a little shadow.

Outside, as always, existence flowed, people running, cars with several angry drivers. Sometimes someone reached out and cursed, someone walked around, confused, a group of girls wearing short miniskirts, with pink and orange hair, added to men's lust and their promiscuity, saw something on a phone, bursting with laughter. He looked up from the hill. It was silent, it had no eyes, no mouth, no gray hair, no white shirt with a wooden collar. Next to that, I looked up to see if that river was there, but no, I was wrong, my eyes were killed by an ugly river of tens of floors of buildings. I started to hate the city that I loved so much, this city of blue seas with kelp shore, with that healing iodine. It lacked infrastructure. Maybe now, as I sit with the curtain, holding it with one hand, someone is bribing someone to build something, bringing the beauty of the city into collapse. What am I saying? As much as I exist, I hate nature, because when I am imagination, I have many friends with her, and she has even promised me an unforgettable trip to some places where she has her wonders. Let's see how long he will keep his word. I opened the door. It hummed again. Everything was in the waterfall of reality, in the river of existence. I closed it again; it seemed as if the same scene was repeated, only that the sun, the source of life, was hidden behind a palace, leaving a part of the city in shadow.

I didn't take the message back to reality. It terrified me. I wanted to go out with nature, but I had to be in my imagination, which, to be transformed, I had to close my eyes. I closed the curtain. Silence and darkness fell in the room again. I threw some wood on the fire; the volume of the flame increased, as if he took a deep breath. My face and clothes turned a flame color. The fluorescent pony faded a little. I refilled the glass with wine, then sat down by the fire that was the only source of life for me alone in this room. I watched as the flames formed strange shapes. Then I closed my eyes, darkness, darkness everywhere. I started to panic. I could not see anything, I could only feel, feel breathing and a cocktail of sweet and quiet sounds that in those moments were dressed with a hiss of terror, when the reality was the opposite. I was happy that something beautiful was happening to me at last and I had my imagination in hand, even though I was so immersed in several layers of imagination, that I had to come out of several dreams to reach awakening, and the sweet voice that called me, which was the only thing I would go back to if I did.

Journey with Nature Through Her Body

Instantly, I had an illusion where I was surrounded by white clouds. The clouds seemed like the frame of what I was seeing, where in the middle there was a dark and wild vortex that was waiting to devour your mind with its flattering gaze. I turned to imagination to snuggle, then I was imagination. Inside the white cloud, which resembled a dream frame, I ran out of energy and my friend, nature, appeared. I was happy. I smiled. A fantastic sight to see and criticize, both for better and for worse.

The biggest sin was talking while seeing that scene where the birds were making love in their free nature. Trees in harmony with their feathers and meandering rivers colored by changing algae. As soon as she felt my presence, that of a pleasant stranger, she took flight some seagulls, some pelicans and then a flock of birds that together formed a lip. The birds were multi-colored, so every part of that lip looked like a rainbow to welcome you in its flattering way, all coming together. Body, soul, mind. Instinctively, I smiled too, waving at him in greeting. Although I sometimes hate imagination, she still knows how to make me her own in many ways, leaving me in the company of many of her friends.

"Nature, what happened to you? Is your scalp damaged?" I asked when she caressed my hair lightly with a white brush that I could feel the freshness of, that made me shiver.

"No, dear, what in your world is dandruff or snow, here is called hail. It is a welcome ritual for a good friend like you, fallen head over heels in the claws of imagination," Nature returned to me. The place had filled with hailstones, hail that gave the place an alternate beauty. The tulip and lilac plots were draped in the most Mother Nature-friendly bridal veil. To my special arrival, this good and dangerous friend gave so much importance to the fields of pearls, in harmony with the white color in this plot, that it seemed as if this hail never stopped. I instantly pictured myself in existence, where I was an Erin holding a blue umbrella in my hand, facing the wind that almost turns the umbrella upside down to make it like a parachute, and people running around getting wet from the hail that fell on people's heads like small pebbles. Cars turn into rivers and pedestrians walk with difficulty because their shoes have soaked in water. An elderly mother with a nose like a pepper was walking along the pavement, a malicious one. I could tell by her look that it was more bitter than an insult, and with a white scarf on her head, her overalls covered with white balls which were so vast that they seemed to pour pitifully into the artificial river, to be wetted into the form of meaningless maps. A stream of hair fell on her cheeks, whose pale white color gave the first impression that she was old. This old woman ran like a marathon runner to get from one side of the road to the other side where some mischievous teenagers and black souls were having fun throwing water away with their car, tearing it in half to wet anyone who was in that brood of ignorance. Their speed was great, but their goal was to raise the water as much as possible to reach the sidewalk to wet the pedestrians. When they approached her and deliberately wet the poor old woman, I immediately opened my eyes in horror, relieved to see my dark room, the sparking fire, and the fluorescent pony hovering as if testifying to the lack of gravity. I was imagining within the imagination. I glanced at the glass of wine that still had some, turned it once, swirled it in my mouth across my palate, savored the sharp, bitter taste, and then closed my eyes with my unprecedented thirst to escape from reality for a little time. A beautiful surprise was waiting for me, and nature was preparing this for me, but I didn't know anything. I was afraid of nature because at the most beautiful moment, it turns the day into a torrential rain where you don't even have time to curse. My friend Nature started the introduction of herself and her divine body faintly; at first she started with a downpour that had her main element. It was so golden, wet, but it didn't create puddles, just a few spots of silver water, that there was nothing more noble and elegant than in all the worlds I had been able to escape to with my mind, like a supersonic train traveling at the speed of light, making the biological clock seem long and stop. This rain, when it fell, at the moment of impact with the head, emitted a sound like several violins together, which made a musical wave so calm that you closed your eyes and absorbed all the benefits of that moment, however little. When it fell on your hair, you quickly felt the moisture, as if the bubbles of water moved downwards by gravity and covered the face at once. The hand of nature was clearly visible, that hand with that touch full of life and full of caresses that increased the desire to live.

"Wait, wait, I still have something for you, my imaginary friend," the wind blows lightly in my ears. Although, I was named Erin, like my ex-girlfriend, yes, a combination of strange coincidences. Again, all my friends, behind closed eyes, called me like that, it's normal that in this world of lineages, I can't be Erin.

"Wait, wait, I still have something for you, my imaginary friend," the wind blows lightly in my ears. Although, I was named Erin, like my ex-girlfriend, yes, a combination of strange coincidences. Again, all my friends behind closed eyes called me like that, it's normal that in this world of lineages, I can't be Erin.

"Why? What skill will you use to win me over by surprising me?" I asked Nature. In an instant, the horizon took on a purple color, which seemed to me like a threat to show me its graces, like a strip stick. It's a color that really surprised me; it had been a long time since I had seen such a color so much that the feelings started to love the brutal and destructive nature. I didn't even know if it existed as a coloring project or not. At least where I am, you see this color in nature too often, to say the least, even in that world full of ingratitude and cruelty, with children who are hungry and thirsty to the point where they get used to their fate, an extreme thirst, as much as I thirst for a glass of wine – ironic for the truth. It made my body shiver where they call me existence with irony. They did me a favor when they left me alone to feel abandoned. Now, in my imagination, I don't bother anyone anymore. It even sends a silent thank you for what they did to me, to feel so abandoned that I decided to sacrifice myself in imagination, like the fire in the fireplace and the fluorescent pony as soon as the light goes out, but his happiness knows that there will be life again at dinner. In the dark.

"Imagination." Nature is calling me, as some playful birds were playing in the clouds and in her hair.

"Yes…" I answered.

"Take a look at this." She tries to surprise me. I was really surprised when this tortuous nature made itself known with a hill, everywhere prevailing a green, in that flat color of grass, as if either someone had cut it in a level manner, or someone had just finished a nature portrait. There were little hills everywhere, where if you walked into one you could see all the little bumps covered in green grass that gave you the feeling that a herd of green-clad blacksmiths had bent over for the season's harvest. Then I noticed a field. A little further, I started up another hill. In the fields where these small hills lay, my eye caught some bushes, since the sun had taken on a slightly rusty color. A few tens of meters on the horizon was a house, which was surrounded by trees several meters high, some enough to create a relaxing and cool shade, so that he could not take his eyes off it.

"What are you doing to me like this, dear Nature?" I said to her as a flattering complaint while she laughed, as if stubbornly, that for a few seconds I didn't like that strong wind straightening my hair.

"Wait, wait, my dear, because you haven't seen anything until now," he tells me. "You have come to me as a friend, and I feel privileged to show you my beauty and my wildness, so that when you go to reality, what are you talking about?" Nature ends. I started to melt completely. Those beautiful views full of freshness scared me, but also calmed me down, because if I told anyone these things, for example Erina, she would turn away from me and run away forever.

"Here is the other one."

From what I could see, we were on some coral reefs, where it looked more like a picturesque peninsula on which there were a number of artists trying with their pens to give life in their own way and progressive style, when in fact they were very backward. Slightly detached was an island, and then several other slightly smaller islands that formed a wonderful archipelago, for want of a better 'word. Far from these islands that were bathed in the blue, blue and purple sea, there appeared a white appearance, which was some white rocks where they were wet with frothy water, as if an egg white had cracked and coagulated its protein. After each wave, the green corals seemed to come to the surface just to get the oxygen they needed.

"Is there more…?" I asked, because I felt startled by the ride that seemed to send me into the open air again under the supersonic train.

"Do you even have to ask?" Nature returns. "This is the most special surprise I have for you. Have you ever seen a geyser?"

"Geyser? What is this?" From this name, I felt like I was in a science fiction fantasy, where the only formula was the courage to see the sequel. In front of us, as if without realizing how we passed, we found ourselves in front of the geyser. A light breeze blew like a spring breeze, while immediately before us appeared the greatest wonder I had ever seen in all the virtual and real worlds. The geyser appeared. It was a small cave, covered in snow everywhere and with a spout at the top that spewed water at a high pressure, while the return camouflaged itself with a suction lure until you could prove you could die in a conscious state for a while longer with suffering. This was a message of beautiful nature, how dangerous it knew how to be.

"Water volcano," I thought, stunned as a provincial. After seeing the wonders that are still in existence, but not maintained, I thought of sitting down somewhere and resting. As I sat down, I thought of the hill with the small hills and the green fields, that house in the shadows of those trees, where the desire said how I would like a house like that, that strange geyser covered with spitting snow water with a high pressure, the coral reefs with those small islands and the purple sea and the white rocks that were wet by the foaming sea. Sitting, with the idea that I was near the geyser, I felt a great heat and a noise, a war of monsters, a war going on below, somewhere in the sub-existence. I became aware when I saw that I was in a volcano, but with real fire this time, and the tops of the mountains seemed to be painted with blood as a loss of virginity. Here, Nature shows a bit of her masochism, the wildness she has in her like the island of Saint Helena.

She introduced me to a waterfall that flowed like a bridal veil. On the sides there were black rocks and some long winter flowers as far as the eye could see. With an infernal speed, faster than that of lightning, enough to make even the bravest adrenalin junkie tremble, I found myself near a lowland, with the trees colored yellow by drought, wide plains followed by a range of mountains. Nature threw me from one part of her body to another, without thinking, without understanding. Only when I saw with delight where I was, did I then reassemble myself, like a jumper who passed through every landscape with the fear of being caught and destroyed by the paladins.

We entered a cave. I was really afraid. The drops of water that fell from above dripped into the river and made an endless sound that broke the peace a little, but that looked like a pentagram notebook with amber notes and music to reawaken the desire once again, to love every part of existence. Inside, there was water like a Victorian carpet where those calm-breaking drops fell, mirror-like rock, and when you looked up, it looked like the rock had melted and then re-frozen, leaving a few pieces like the tip of an upside-down knife. It was beautiful, but terrifying; it seemed as if nature was showing me its wild beauty. After leaving the cave, we kayaked in the middle of a river valley. I had never seen so much beauty. A river meandered between two short but huge hills several kilometers long. Their faces were covered with fossils green that looked like mold, and in places it had the shape of a black cloud. This caused the river to hold in its bed an indescribable shadow of beauty.

The sound that the water made every time I pushed forward

with the paddle and those light lines, like benevolent waves, gave you a special feeling, as if you felt that beneath you the lost souls were reawakening to go on their journey toward a butterfly, toward a flower, toward a baby, where they were actually describing the life of the grave, punishment until the day of judgment. After a small island with a strange shape, like a goose leg, where I suddenly found myself, Nature surprised me when it took me to another dimension of its physical and spiritual beauty where I was speechless. Here, this nature was exciting me with her body, which were those unseen images to the point that I thought he should immediately make love to her. I had never seen the glacial lake.

A place of trees whose branches were dry and white with frost, some trees from green turned gray by snow crystals, and then a white lake with pieces of ice floating, as if patrolling its bed. After this miracle, we went to a canyon, the eighth wonder of the world, bare trees with few leaves, and some hills where the separation was not a field, but an abyss, sometimes small, sometimes very deep from the top of the rocks and sometimes passionate, to weave an unforgettable poem. There was no field, but a large pit which separated the rocks from one another. We spent the rest of the day looking at red sand deserts and high dunes where occasional storms warned us to take care of our eyes. It was the hottest place, but not as much as Danakil in Ethiopia. I saw a field where there was a reservoir and a horse grazing peacefully. We gazed at the old mole mountains, some mountains stuck in the shape of apples on top and a calm lake soaked my feet. I saw some bays with those irregular arches caused by the water which crashed with force and fell, foaming. I was amazed when I was on top of a new ridge, where there was snow on one side of a knife-like peak where I sat, mesmerized, high up in confusion, thinking that this could not be imagination, not real, not real, nothing, when really it was all just a matter of seconds. But, for the last time, I wanted to see once again that small hill that spouted water under pressure from the bottom to the top. I stared at this sight for hours. Pshshsh... fufufu, pshshsh... fufufu... was the sound the water made when it came out of the mouth and fell, half into the steamy air, the rest below. Its side had a beautiful appearance and menacing attitude, full of smiles and pushes for curiosity as you approached. This was the most beautiful natural fountain I had ever imagined, but also the most dangerous. After the cruel and beautiful geyser... and his fu-fu, where in reality my snores were. I fell asleep as always. I returned to this quiet world where the opposite of relativity is the absolute. I didn't like anything. I closed my eyes and opened them again, disgusted with where I was and all this hatred for reality that had been given to me by the situation I was in. I felt drops of water on my face, falling like pieces of ice stalactites, melting on my chest, making me feel a shiver. This whole journey was simply to show God's greatness to every creation in harmony that He had created.

Advice from a glass of wine

The fire was almost completely extinguished, and with the death of the fire, a new feeling was born, burning more than the fire. A feeling not like mothers who have beautiful children and abandon them in the trash, but like mothers who have ugly children and love them more every day. How many times would your fire sacrifice itself for me to awaken an earthly spiritual state? The cushion I was sitting on had lost all of its power, making me feel like I was sitting on cold cement. I was taken, I was numb. I wasn't picking myself up since that blink before blurs me out. I was drunk.

Walking toward the winery to get another bottle of red wine, the next surprise occurred to me. In reality, I never knew what a geyser was, or I never knew the geographical names of nature. I never knew there was a geyser, I never even heard of it anywhere. What I didn't understand was how the paranormal had penetrated in my fragile mind and had introduced me to that precious information. Nature drove me with her class, sometimes wild, sometimes gentle, sometimes calm and sometimes crazy, sometimes devious, insidious, sly, clever. More, she had flattered me into her illusions, and then used me to find out what she contains in that further world, that world where one mind does not imagine it as another mind, where there is diversity of people, because the mind and what it thinks and imagines makes the difference between intelligence and short mind. I'm glad that my prestige world mind has colors and variety of things unseen from other worlds, because every world is different and unique. When I am with my eyes open, I invite people to enter my world, but when they come out, they are no longer myself, so without anyone pitying me for not understanding my world, I entered the worlds of others, but not to inspect what is there in depth, but to explain to you what kind of world is mine.

A person with many worlds is a person with many possibilities of choices, with many possibilities of deviations. A smart person he is, if he handles his intelligent information well; a world is made into a mind. I grab the bottle from the enoteca and head straight for the glass to join us and have a little lightning talk. As soon as the door opener made the opening sound, the eyes opened and began to widen. There was no light, so the unicorn pony was still hovering, and his tail was pink and his long hair was the same color. There was charm. As soon as I did the rite based on tasting the wine, I flashed it once, flashed it and once again, after drinking it, I looked at the glass with a variety of sensitive glances. It seemed to me that a pair of eyes lifted the glass and were watching me, as if behind a steamed-over glass in the bathroom. From this moment of silence and solitude, I needed a friend the most, a friend who knows how to keep secrets and who only gives a taste of pleasure everywhere, but a friend who knows how to look you in the eye when he speaks, no, be a master of listening.

"Oh, my glass, my glass, only you are standing next to me, you look me in the eyes when you talk, and you don't make a sound when I think."

"It would be a lack of dignity for a glass that holds the classic liquid inside if I don't blur your feelings a little," he returns, my glass. What a voice she had, the emotion she expressed when she spoke, what attitude she held; she was the queen of the golden times.

"How is it possible that I can't tell him what he feels?" And I looked at the fluorescent pony and the fire that had died. The pony had triumphed.

"It's quite clear, you don't have the courage to be frank." After saying these words to me, the liquid swirled around the glass like a ballerina doing a mesmerizing swan dance.

"I can't find the courage, my dear, to talk to her and express to her what she feels. It seems to me that she doesn't understand me, I just sit and wait for a message that I receive to start expressing my world to her world. The world that I think might go away once it knows that I own it like this."

"If you want to have me as your friend, you will never have to do anything about real feelings. I will never find the courage you lack. Don't like your world? Enter her world and destroy it. Invite him into your world and explain everything. Maybe it can be the first stage of a love, like the first day."

"I dont know what to do."

"Quite simply, hurt me and love the girl of the white stripes. Erin. I felt her lips, they are soft and exciting enough to make me blush with embarrassment. I intoxicate you with my juice, and the thoughts that come from a troubled feeling I wear with sincerity."

"Yes, exactly what do I do with Erina?"

"I don't know, maybe you can merge and make a single body."

"Their body and ignorance to unite hurts me more than ever."

"Dear Erin, don't think that you have been abandoned by everyone. On the contrary, think that even if they leave you, it is because they are afraid of your wide world that made them know their narrow world."

"What should I think?"

"Something more real. Drink until agony. If someone comes for you is the moment to know who loves your world and is not afraid of the world you own. If you die, this world was not for you. Go for another one."

"Are you scolding me?"

"No. I'm making you get drunk and be as generous as possible with your feelings. Free yourself from the null cables that have conquered you, and then be comfortable. Be sure that you don't drink the next glass out of stress, but out of fun. and the great love you have for those around you. Don't forget, my dear, that forbidden things excite you more. I am prohibited for you, by Koranic order, but you love me."

"What do I do now? I seem to be ending, I'm becoming like the fire that went out. I want to stay in the hand of the air, in the middle of the illusions, in the middle of the mercy to see the tree, just like the pink unicorn that is in the mercy of the night."

"The pink unicorn is born when the light dies and dies when the source of life arises."

"It is a form of survival instinct."

"You are wrong," scolds the glass of wine. "It is built to be clear. To make the first impact with its uniqueness, and then to be an ordinary fluorescent object."

"What do I do to be good? Teach me, because it seems to me that you are devouring me with your fine contours, not me, you. You pissed me off and now you're getting an honest confession out of my deep-seated feelings."

"Unify yourself. Others love you, you're the one who doesn't love them. You're a narcissist for the world you have, you're happy with yourself, so slow down, while you're immersed in parentheses and talk to a worthless thing that serve only the luxurious taste, that class who have consciously sold the eternal for the temporary."

Suddenly, I felt that I had drunk all that was in the glass. She was right, I need to be more open to everything that surrounds me, I need to express what I think, be frank with my feelings, unify with myself, as the glass of wine beautifully said. But I still think I'm not ready to express myself. What nonsense, reality does not exist.

The War of Nature

In the background, suddenly, like a music covered with a cloak to seem invisible, but above all strange, a light rhythm was heard; very extravagant, quite sincere notes that played together like three birds that sit in a tree and sing wildly. In the end, the result is a variety of colors of notes and a priceless feeling that there is no auction and buyer who can have enough wealth to buy it. It was strange, except for seven notes, like an inexperienced musician. I also noticed other notes, which were not marked on the pentagram. I leaned on the seat of the armchair, filled the wine glass with my delicate hand and fingers, closed my eyes and prayed to the gaze not to part with the starry candles, the light and the beautiful night life, that heavenly organ, which does not always appear with a body. The music was heard quite softly entering the sweet ear canals, relaxing me under its panoramic sounds, as if I were under the effect of a drug. The black background and the fire made the walls seem to wave every time it took on great power. The glass of wine was silent. My feelings woke up again, and what tormented me was no longer the courage to go and tell two words to her, but will she be able to wake up like always, glass in hand, rocking in my chair, cushions on the floor that are colorful even in the dark? I closed my eyes. Even though I had closed them, I instantly found myself in a war of imaginations, endless galaxies swirling around each other and strange people who seemed to dance to a worthless pagan rhythm, who were no longer called as they are today.

The fabulous landscape was a miracle that the eye can see, but what if only the mind is seeing this? A narrow one-lane road wound through several village quarters; the road was covered in golden leaves because it was autumn. On either side, beige trees stripped of their finery and costume, their finesse already gone by the wayside for a while now. The tree held a classy look, a smile on every branch of irony, and a playful movement that made the wind so visible to the human eye that you could touch it. On the left side was a Dutch mill, surrounded everywhere with a green field, where the oriental tranquility that this plot had made the soul hardly come out to experience these images being more present. On the other hand, there was no Dutch mill, but trees bare to the utmost insolence, white trees that seemed to live in black times, a bitter cold, a frost, and an unimaginable coolness, different from the another of calmness and relaxation that represented a world full of colors, colors everywhere. This war of landscapes was separated by the only stretched beauty, the road, sometimes covered with rusty petals, sometimes with frozen and dead petals. Without a sound, the road with its beautified ridge sat quietly, listening to the frosty weather, which, ironically for the mirages of beauty and tranquility, was very noisy. In the middle of this landscape, I sat looking at the only thing I wanted to see, myself from behind, naked, and the yellow road dressed in a dress of fallen petals, which embellished its contours and the whiteness of the cold wind. They waged a war of extremes, the evil weather, white and glittering, pelting them with plumes of white wind and frozen, lifeless leaves, while the green side with Dutch mills stood silent, only watching the aggression of its friend. Very soon, the yellow sun will punish her; the end, the judgments of nature are there, in the fiery globe that is now only in its youth.

Then I heard a louder crash, a branch snapping mercilessly, sending everything crashing down onto my face, like a slap from a liquid but strangely cold hand. I opened my eyes. The room was the same darkness that it was a few seconds ago, the music with its ghostly notes that made you feel the miracle on the chair, while what broke this whole illusion of a closed door was the open door that was rustling while the cold wind beat my face. Its power and the death of the touch sensors from the cold made me no longer feel the glass of wine as it almost fell to the ground. It was very strange what happened in reality. My imagination explained to me in its own way that diversity of colors and diversity of feelings. She would tell me to be careful. I would tell her back, "Leave me alone, I'm impressed."

Beyond Imagination

I didn't know where I was anymore. Everything was such a mess that I didn't know how I was going to get through it, but I knew who I was, yes, yes, I was... wait, I've met myself now. I forgot that I am with many inter-imaginary personalities, I am a double, triple person, I know. Thinking like this, I expect to get approval from the real reality, which does not belong to even some kind of existing world, so until now, I live a non-existent, irrational life. I was a river that has no real flow. I want to be again. Me gaining myself. Anyway, that's the beauty when you live irrationally through different dream concepts, everything you do as you want it to be, a world of dark color in golden colors and you get to be the critic, to be the sovereign, the powerful, the king, although there are many on Earth who, like spoiled children, enjoy these titles, but one is divine, he is the almighty God who is one.

You have everything in your hands, you can even imagine a landscape in your mind, then you paint it with illusions, with the brush that are the closed eyelashes of the eye to feel the lust of the beautiful thing. I'm already painting an image, to everyone's anger, rather of the universe, of space, of nature, of myself, of friends, of the glass of wine that was broken, of the sun that seems to me not to warm me, but to cool me. What's wrong with you, why are you frowning? Look, your hydrogen turned into nitrogen, you are a pity, even the moon is laughing at you, look how friendly the planetary world is with you, and why? You are nothingness in the cold, and peace in the warmth. Because you already cannot satiate some worlds with your will, but with other extremes, with other fluctuations of thoughts. But don't be sad, because we need each other, let the moon frown, she is cynical because she knows the ability and the damage of its absence. It lives at night, hiding in its scant light during the day and hovering over our heads, watching us, like a pony waiting for the capitulation of the chimney. What we accept is the night sun. I left the house as usual in the usual and elegant clothes. Parisians keep to themselves. I put on my light-colored glasses and cycled straight to a destination I had just created. It was an innocent destination to be trampled by the wheels of my bicycle. That virgin world of bright colors would have wanted to preserve its honor more than to be trampled by a finisher like me, who wasn't even me at all. But my pleasure is greater than her love of having an intact body, and she does not know that. It is my creature and I do what I want with it. The path was surrounded on both sides by a red river, in which some beautiful and quite radiant nymphs floated like fish thirsty for air, but predatory, hypnotizing and with an insidious allure.

They swam from both sides, just like me. We were in sync. Sometimes, I even thought that they should smile, so I did and they responded to my whims of my mind. The road was yellow, fallen leaves everywhere on both sides. Trees, sometimes stripped of the treacherous leaves of the season and made ashamed of their nakedness, sometimes dressed in chic clothing full of blue, stood by the side of the road with pride. Ahead of me was a white mountain. Its green trees had taken on a dual color, both white and green, making it look even more like the legs of the still creature's white shirt. The bike seemed to me to be going at breakneck speed. My hair was left behind and the disfigurement was inevitable to the point of ugliness. Then I would pass through a park with tall, dense pines, a bad road, and me on my bike, pushing myself through such thickets with the hyperbolizing speed of light. That day, my imagination took me to walk on the sea, to play with the sharks, with the long-nosed and charming dolphins and to talk intimate things with the fishes nearby. When I was walking alone on the side of a sharp-pointed canyon, I remembered that everything had gotten out of my control. I looked to the left; there were only flowers of one color. It seemed to me that at that moment I was in the gardens of Madagascar, the famous shores that did not make you run away. But still, my thoughts were clouded. On the other hand, the slow reality where you can't do as you please. Erina cutting some fruit wearing a transparent red robe.

What I needed now was to go for a bike ride with Erina through a road covered with red leaves, with trees everywhere on the sides, covering the road with their shadows, and with seas and oceans on both sides, giving the situation freshness and the right noise for the atmosphere. Suddenly, Erina appeared because I wanted her to, her hair flowing like a great ocean wave. Some green tints in her black hair looked like surfers trying to challenge her strong and wild beauty. Her small nose, her lips like a cluster of petals recently plucked from a tree, her neck like a branch of a tree, while her shoulders were so small that they made me see clearly this beauty that I did not know I had, that I created. I think I fell in love.

"Erina," I called with a voice that I had never imagined. I was scared, because in my mind I heard other voices that were telling me something, but I didn't understand them. Maybe someone wanted to scold me because I was in an intergalactic world where even I didn't know what I was thinking anymore.

"Did you want to tell me something?" She turned to me,

turning her head slightly to the right where I was. At that moment, the road had taken the shape of Erina's body and we were walking on top of it. Surprisingly, she only pedaled without feeling pain. That body that I imagined as such, it was good to be one of the rings of Saturn.

"No, no, nothing. Leave it alone." I became confused, as her body and the tire of the bicycle touched erogenous zones that made Erina moan, unheard, once. Not like those moans when we made love by the fire. She glared at me. Although she was wild, in that peaceful nature with seas and oceans, her power lived. Saturn's rings, better.

"Do you think you can make fun of me?"

"I am afraid of the ability to mock," I return, embarrassed.

"Why?"

"Because it is very complicated as a game."

"As much as you? Your closure, your loneliness that has put a big sign where it says to open or not to open Erin at all?" she asks me, pedaling faster than the speed of light. We no longer had any units of measurement for speed. The only alternative for our distances was the light years that seemed to us not trillions of kilometers, but very close.

"Maybe less." I started to follow him like crazy. The speed had exceeded that of sound and everything seemed as if within a second we saw something we had passed twice.

"I see, you want to be the first in this game of horrors, swans and imaginative creatures?"

"Why, do you feel where you are?"

"Yes. I am in a world for someone to invite me for a walk and tell me a special feeling. I'm touching hesitation."

"Does it look like that to you?" Now, our speed was so great that, behind us, we left a line of hot but blue fire. In the space where we almost went to the Milky Way, I met someone who was bathing there like an Olympic swimmer. Imagination was on alert. I had passed the targets.

"Yes. I even feel strange, as if a metamorphosis is going through my body," he told me. She closed her eyes and opened her arms.

"Maybe when he closes his eyes, the truth that we fear will happen."

"Exactly, because when I open them, in front of me in a dark room slightly lit by a faint flame is you with your eyes closed and writhing."

"Erina, please return to my imagination."

"I am your dream, did you forget? Or did I simply move into the past?"

"Hmm, maybe," I returned. Already, the blue flame that roared behind us, which was burning behind us, died out, giving way to a surprisingly cold red flame. Apparently, our hearts were mistakenly ignited with a cold fire that was supposed to consume us. I was terrified because everything I was creating terrified me.

"You are very lukewarm at wrong moments," she told me.

"Are you telling me to burn at the right moment?"

"That I have your feeling in my hand, I have in my hand what I feel for you."

"Are you afraid of me?" I asked him, and the speed was already so high that our stomachs started to feel queasy, and it seemed as if we were losing our senses and as if we were falling from a great height from time to time.

"Yes, sort of. Your behavior. It seems to me that you have no recourse in yourself."

"Why?"

Both of us, even though we were moving at a speed

undetectable by terrestrial radars, our eyes were on each other, not on the world of ice we had entered, and where the stars were so close that I could take one, and give it to my Erina, loving and fiery like an illuminated bouquet, but I didn't want to manifest strange sensations right here in the unknown world.

"I fear strange people," he told me. "They terrify me."

"Even when I don't have the courage to act like a weirdo?"

"Anyway, I continue to fear you, every time more. How many times have I seen you in your silence?"

"I would like to express that…"

"Not the brats from your worlds where you sit and snuggle for hours."

"The world will give it to you, dear. Do you want it? It is as cruel as it is beautiful. You need courage to accept it and be present in it."

"What was this?"

"Love." I returned it boldly.

"Love is a temporary feeling," she returned it.

"Temporary, permanent."

"Permanent, unknown."

"Invisible stranger, to stay by your side." I started playing with words.

"Incomplete attendance," he told me and it seemed as if he possessed me.

"I feel like I'm losing this game."

"No, you won the game, but you're losing a lot of ground. Look, even your speed has dropped to thousands of kilometers per second, from several hundreds of thousands."

"It is dangerous to walk slowly."

"You yourself created the dangerousness. Now, give your dry blood the adrenalin of drug addicts. Are you afraid to slip into my feelings of love?"

"No, but…"

"You find the courage, the girl's heart is like the ocean that plays with the surfers. They raise big waves, excite you, attract you, let them slide on your body. If they liked it, let them go to the shore, if not, throw for the sharks. But if you fall from the surf, I will pick you up again. A woman's pleasure when she knocks a man off her is to make sure, until the shark eats it all up and makes sure they're screaming in pain."

"You made this sacrifice for me?" I asked him and immediately felt a change coming from outside my imagination.

"Getting others to love you, is it a sacrifice?"

"I do not know. That's how it looks."

"Hurry up, dear, as we have no time to waste. The world is ending, so we'll have to stop then."

"You do this for me?" I asked him, awakening once again a feeling of love, not for him, but for myself. When you fall in love every day, you forget what love is.

"Yes."

"Unconditionally?"

"No," he returns to me. I was silent. My world that I had created was falling down on me. She smiled as she pedaled so hard it seemed impossible.

"Are you trying to get away from me?"

"The world is ending, catch it. Then I'm yours," he told me and from there a strange race started. "I could set a trap for you with a single thought."

"This is the condition?" I ask him.

"No." He gives me a smile.

"What do you mean?"

"Finding, catching a woman is an indecipherable mystery. If

you catch it, you have to decipher it. Then you can love it. This is the passport for you. Without this, you will not know how to love."

"No, I cannot. The feeling finished me, the world swallowed me, you defeated me."

"Coward."

"Somewhat."

"Cynic?"

"I grew up. You're right, I'm a coward."

"Are you afraid to try to love me, because the idea of fear of falling, or of not being able to decipher me has entered your blood?"

"I am a knight of illusionary thoughts, who control my own."

"I am the jockey, who has prestige as a horse and mirage as a field, who in the end wins the race."

"I didn't say you beat me yet."

"Love me?"

"Yeah, a lot. Even before I knew you, I felt that I would love you."

"You see, you didn't slip."

"I like you, but I'm afraid to love you."

"What do you mean?"

"I lack the class to express myself. I feel like my warmth is turning me into a snob."

"You also lack class in thinking."

"I noticed it."

"Class is not needed to make a girl feel for you, but to like something about you. As for love, the heart needs courage."

"You love me?" Here, I broke the thick glass of ice that wrapped courage. That glass from which I was in this situation. Lost.

"I like you, let's say."

"You are taking revenge."

"No, we just drew."

"But we cannot leave this adventure like that."

"I want to go beyond eternity. Can you do it?"

"We have already done it. Look, we are on Venus."

"Eternity is temporary in reality. In imagination, permanent and unique."

"Where are we?"

"It can't be anything, we are in a world that I imagined that beat your world. Look, everything is burning."

"We are already between two worlds?" Erina, after I said that sentence all fear, saw me all anger. "Then, we have both slipped."

"Yes."

"How will we get up?"

"Let's find the courage." She laughed with a smug chuckle. "Everything about us looked the best."

"What do you mean?"

"We are alone. We can make love without falling. I can make love with Jupiter, you with the moon, and thus, we escape from the fall that you fear so much."

"Help is a feeling that originates from the fighting spirit," I said.

Suddenly, I found myself in my own world. Erina had only tested me by defeating me with her imagination. We were already walking at billions of kilometers per second and everywhere we had different trees and animals, and that cold fire that followed us from behind.

"Did you say that we had fallen on the neck in that element that was not shared with us?"

"We are not fighting anymore. I opened the way for you," Erina tells me with her lustful voice. It seemed that something inside her wanted and I had it.

"We are simply becoming a body," I returned and started to get excited.

"Yes."

It turns me serious. "I can't, goodbye."

She turned to me and said, "I would love you, if you would give it to me as a joke, but you can't give up your obsession with imagination."

"I lost."

"You still have finesse in your soul. Use it, dear."

"I died with my being, along with the finesse inside."

"Farewell to you who cannot find an iota of fire in your cold walls of your strange heart."

"Love you."

"Time out. Back to reality. Your world made our hair stand on end."

"You are right, to love and ask to be loved. It was like an adrenalin never experienced before. Goodbye, my strange world."

Just Three Minutes

Terror ran through my veins. I couldn't find the slightest bit of courage to re-enter reality, that feeling where everything is burning with a fire that requires supernatural power. Imagine what a world that is. Where to shut the doors mercilessly? With thousands of worlds in my mind, I don't know which one to choose, to be who I have been, or would it be better not to be who I am at all? But who will I be? I have to choose a name for myself that I have lost. Losing yourself in the middle of the day is like trying to challenge the phosphorescent eyes of a cat in the middle of the night. I was walking down the dark road of thoughts. I tried not to talk to myself, but the spirit was sloppy in those moments; it got out of my control, making me suffer at least because he was chaste. Here his chastity slipped from my lips and fell in an unknown place, in a wet place, on a day that has wet the whole Earth with a torrential rain. Unprecedented chastity, like an illusion, left my body and joined a stream of dirty water, quite depraved. I did not call him, as the rivers of promiscuous waters urge you not to listen to outside voices. They want you to hear only the gurgling sound of extreme erosion, deafening straight into the darkness. As a person without a soul, I started on my invisible road, where its landscape rode through the mirages of illusions, introducing me to a world even more suggestive, wonderful and moreover unknown. How valuable is the unknown in the invisible worlds? The road was dry, there was a pleasant glow of red dust, there was a strong wind, but she looked like she was made of resin and did not move. Everything was out of my hands. From above, when you raised your head, you saw huge bees, not like those of the mysterious island of Vern, but even bigger, moving at a speed that seemed to tire you when you saw them. It was a speed where the limit of the most, the smallest, the slowest, took shape and life. Those large, multi-colored, long-winged creatures that stopped in some small trees, that looked as if they were falling on eggs when they landed, walked so slowly that you were amazed. You had the opportunity to see a strange miracle for so long, but also the mechanics they followed when they walked.

The kinetic force for them was non-existent before. I don't know what physics they used for their bodies, so big and smooth, moving so slowly. I saw the bees and the small trees where those traveling creatures, tourists of only twenty days of life, were, and I saw the gloomy sky with sparkles, the glass of wine that vibrated. As I walked, the earth gradually changed, made other plans showing her wildness, then everything was calm, making you taste the glass of wine inserted between her long, slender fingers, full of grace and class. I was drinking and slurping down a delicious drink. Everything seemed to be in place. On the sidewalks, I was always accompanied by mystical, beautiful, happy creatures. I saw several types of gypsies. I saw the kings of tuna, Erin, the girl of the white stripes, who was a body, and myself, walking straight with visionary sight, straight to the world of pathetic illusion. I shouted once so that no one could hear, but no one listened to me, all of us heroes of ourselves, and our selfishness was exactly where we should not be, in our imaginary worlds, stubbornly telling ourselves what few have the ability to tell where they can go. Everyone was in his imagination; even myself, who had gotten out of control, seemed very controlled because he walked darkly and deep in thought. To go to the other side of personal thoughts, there was no possibility. Even though we saw each other, we showed a reckless indifference that didn't suit us anyway. We were separated only by a thin transparent membrane, but cloudy; it was that plasma that separated the worlds, separated the characters, the prestige, the mirages, the illusions, the contractions, influences, and everything that we thought united us. But what you saw now, you no longer had a guarantee that you would be able to see after even a blink of the eyelids. Because the whole scene is the description, within which there is only one glimpse.

The alternate closing of my eyes filled me with every vision and put me into a world where there were narrow roads in one place and wide ones in another. Precisely, I was in a coffee plot, where its branches were so thick that they also showed aging by giving it a romantic environment that made you feel sensitive, as you felt the aroma of caffeine penetrating through the nasal cavities. To wonder and wonder, a heavy snow fell, where a hair covered thousands of acres of land, lighting up that coffee plot with its whiteness, like a strong neon light. I forgot that I was in the world of waiting and permanent inviolability, I forgot that here everything is not as I thought. The snow was above my head, and the bees, who looked very angry and wanted to sting me, were all no more than a few inches away, and this wonderful natural phenomenon was proceeding with a slowness that seemed like someone with a remote control had stopped the figure, so much so that it looked as if it was gray with old age before, until the snow fell to the ground.

The swirling whiteness hung over my head like a massive cloud. I saw it but I kept walking on a path that I didn't even know where I was going. I had become like the pilgrims in the clouds of thick smoke, who do not even know what they want, what they say, what they are going to do, nor where they are going. On the other hand, it was a world of mess. It was beautiful. I liked it. We were separated again by that ruptured membrane, but this time, I was going from one thought to the next, feeling like my own boss for the first time. So, I was the master of my own thoughts and the knight through the imagination of my own making. The tangled world was beautiful, not disgusting. It was a little different from the other worlds, more different than the world I was in a moment ago, in those big slow-moving bees, where the weather was good, but the road was wet with leaves. In this kind of illusion, the wings changed. It was raining terribly, surrounded by rain creatures and colorful rose petals, but the ground was dry, asphalt, dusty, unscathed. While I was amazed by my imaginations, which took me from one world to another, from imagination to reality, I felt a hand that bit very hard. In the world of the lonely, in the world of fleeting concepts, I felt something soft smoothing my shoulder. I turned my head in horror. As if with vague contours and with a whitened appearance, as if a dream had consumed me, I noticed the indescribable angelic face of Erina, who had a glass of water in her hand and a spear piercing my shoulder. Oh, how beautiful it was. How I longed for him. How much I wanted to touch him, how much I wanted to caress him, tell him all the sweetness in my soul that I felt for him, dare to at least love him for dozens of times.

"Erin." She spoke to me in a soft melodious voice, as if it was coming from three other voices, a little fainter than the first. I continued to feel an exciting blow on the shoulder, a swing, and my wet blouse. There was already a terrible smell and the bees were passing me at such a high speed, as if in alarm that my heart almost stopped in fear as the adrenaline fired up my whole body, to the point where I began to regain the feeling of my body. I felt like I was in danger, I wanted more than ever to take you away from this dream; my imagination had gone wild, but much softer than before.

"Erin." I heard the voice that called me with a rainbow of sounds, touched me, shook me, licked my hot soft cheeks.

"Erin," the voice screamed once more. A bee came close to me, stung me furiously in the face, causing me to wake up from that deep sleep, screaming and startling. My heart was beating fast, my breathing was fast, my eyes were half open, while I still didn't know what had happened to me. I was drenched in sweat and had just escaped the collapse of a large building.

"Erin. Are you OK, dear? I'm terribly terrified."

I turned my eyes, saw the miracle and could not believe my eyes. She was there, sitting by my head, calling me. In short, Erina saved me from those strange creatures, from those steep mountains, from those red seas, and from those nymphs who wanted me to betray, with the beauty of their bodies, honesty, only with a slap that seemed to me as if, in my imagination, one of those bees hit me, when in fact it was a powerful, merciless prick of Erin.

"Oh, Erina, it was you..." How happy I feel, but surprisingly very tired.

"Are you feeling well?" she asked me and sat next to me with anxious eyes and from time to time grabbed my forehead and cheeks, wiping the sweat and water that she had spilled on my face to wake me up. She looked terrified.

"I don't know, my cheek hurt a lot, that giant bee crashed mercilessly on my cheeks," I said, confused, because I was still confused.

"My beautiful one, what bee are you talking about? About the spear that I shot to bring you to the balance from the convulsions that had conquered you, or the piercing of this spear?" I glanced over at Erina, she was smiling, her pouty lips making her look even more adorable.

"What happened?" My voice was faint, lowered to the maximum that it could barely be heard, and sometimes I even spoke with interruptions, as the words did not come out as complete, oratorically, as I really was.

"You lit the fireplace, while sitting next to it with a glass of wine in hand. Then I noticed from the kitchen, where I was preparing a plate of dried fruits to accompany the wine, that you had hung your head and were sleeping. I didn't want to spoil that angelic look of yours, because you know I fall in love all over again when I see your round face, sleeping like an innocent child. You started to growl, which you don't do often. The glass of wine fell from your hand, then you started to shake your head from left to right. With your hands and feet you started to make gestures as if you wanted to remove something that was bothering you. You spoke, something I didn't understand. To be honest, I was scared. That's why I came to wake you up, to stop you from suffering because I saw that you were having a bad dream."

I grabbed Erina's hands and kissed them, intertwined my long fingers with hers, squeezing her hand as hard as I could. I looked around. The environment was romantic – candles, the phone at the head of the bed, which was still ringing, the wine glass was knocked down, the fire was going down and a plate of dried fruits, which my dear Erina had brought me to enjoy as much as possible wine to drink.

"My sober life, what time is it?" I asked in a slightly normalized voice and started to feel good that it was just a terrible dream and nothing is real.

"It's 14:26 minutes, my soul."

"Really? I only slept for three minutes?"

"Yes. You told me to make a plate of fruit and come to you to finish the summer by the fireplace. Then you squirmed. Look what I'm wearing for you." She walked up, advertising her delicious body.

"Oh God, what a horror."

"What?"

"Oh, Erina, long story. It would take me three days to explain what happened to me in those three minutes of sleep."

While I was talking, she was filling the glasses with wine. He slowly came closer, kissed my licked cheek, ran his fingers through my hair and pulled me close to him, all lust. I had removed a lot today. Erina was with me and even loved me. What a terrible world to explain to a beautiful world like Erina. Both of us, leaning on each other, expressing our love with looks, kisses and touches, holding each other with a glass of wine in one hand and a plate of fruit on the floor, the fire drenching our wet faces with hot flames, we started. We experienced the pleasures that the spontaneous moment gave us. She was very beautiful. Even, sometimes, I asked myself, do I deserve this girl? Despite all the real miracles, I began to think about what I had done in such a short time. I had been able to manipulate imagination into reality, but also reality into imagination. I had won.

"Why are you thinking that you are staring at the fire as if you want to swallow it? Don't you feel like doing something crazy after a crazy dream?" He got on top of me

"If that fire is hotter than the love I have for you, but I believe, I burn that fire with that feeling." The fork came off the plate and fell to the floor. Meanwhile, the glass of wine was spilled, spreading across the carpet quickly, creating a stain that

I didn't want to know was ruining my oriental rug. The fire was the witness of our burning desires. That day, it didn't end like that… and everything was real.

END